THE FORCE IS WITH THEM . . .

JACEN loves living things. He keeps pets of all species: animals, plants, insects (some easier to care for than others . . .) and he suspects he can speak to them using the Force . . . though he doesn't quite know how.

JAINA takes after her father, Han. She is a mechanical whiz, always dismantling droids, machines, anything she can get her hands on. Like Han, her spirit and self-confidence sometimes get her into trouble.

LOWBACCA, or "Lowie," is the Wookiee nephew of Chewbacca and a native of the planet Kashyyyk. Taller than any of the others, he loves to climb to the top of Yavin 4's massive jungle trees. And on his belt, he wears . . .

EM TEEDEE, a translator droid built by Chewbacca to convert Wookiee speech to Basic. But because Em Teedee was programmed by See-Threepio, he tends to talk more than he has to.

TENEL KA is the tough, self-sufficient daughter of Teneniel Djo, one of the witches of Dathomir. Loyal, though a little humorless, she will fight beside her friends whenever they find themselves in tough situations.

This book also contains a special sneak preview of the next *Star Wars: Young Jedi Knights* adventure:

LIGHTSABERS

ABOUT THE AUTHORS

KEVIN J. ANDERSON and his wife, **REBECCA MOESTA**, have been involved in many STAR WARS projects. Together, they are writing the six volumes of the YOUNG JEDI KNIGHTS saga for young adults, as well as creating the JUNIOR JEDI KNIGHTS series for younger readers. They are also writing a series of illustrated science books for first and second graders—the STAR WARS COSMIC SCIENCE series—and pop-up books showcasing the Cantina scene and the Jabba's Palace scene.

Kevin J. Anderson is also the author of the STAR WARS: JEDI ACADEMY trilogy, the novel *Darksaber*, and the comic series DARK LORDS OF THE SITH with Tom Veitch for Dark Horse comics. His young adult fantasy novel, *Born of Elven Blood*, written with John Betancourt, was recently published by Atheneum. He has edited several STAR WARS anthologies, including *Tales From the Mos Eisley Cantina* (July 1995), in which Rebecca Moesta has a story.

STAR WARS
YOUNG JEDI KNIGHTS

THE LOST ONES

KEVIN J. ANDERSON
and REBECCA MOESTA

BOULEVARD BOOKS, NEW YORK

STAR WARS: YOUNG JEDI KNIGHTS
THE LOST ONES

A Boulevard Book / published by arrangement with
Lucasfilm Ltd.

PRINTING HISTORY
Boulevard edition / December 1995

All rights reserved.
®, ™ & Copyright © 1995 by Lucasfilm Ltd.
Material excerpted from LIGHTSABERS
copyright © 1995 by Lucasfilm Ltd.
This book may not be reproduced in whole or in part,
by mimeograph or any other means, without permission.
For information address: The Berkley Publishing Group,
200 Madison Avenue, New York, New York 10016.

ISBN: 1-57297-052-9

BOULEVARD
Boulevard Books are published by The Berkley Publishing Group,
200 Madison Avenue, New York, New York 10016.
BOULEVARD and the "B" design
are trademarks belonging to The Berkley Publishing Group.

PRINTED IN THE UNITED STATES OF AMERICA

10 9 8 7 6 5 4 3 2 1

To our editor Ginjer Buchanan,
for her support and enthusiasm,
which made this entire project possible
in the first place, and for extending the series
to let us tell the whole story
. . . and for just being a really neat person.

acknowledgments

To Lillie E. Mitchell, for her fast and furious typing; Jonathan MacGregor Cowan, for being our test reader and providing youthful excitement; Karen Haber and Robert Silverberg, for allowing us to mangle their monickers (sort of); Sue Rostoni and Lucy Wilson at Lucasfilm Licensing, for their sharp eyes and helpful suggestions . . . and Norys Davila at Walt Disney World Celebrity Programs, for having such a nifty first name we couldn't resist using it.

1

AS THE JEWEL-GREEN moon of Yavin 4 dwindled behind them in the *Millennium Falcon*'s rear viewscreens, Jaina Solo gave a happy sigh. "Excited to be going back home, Jacen?" she asked, looking into the liquid brown eyes of her twin brother.

Jacen ran long fingers through his tousled brown curls. "Never thought I'd say it," he admitted, "but a month on Coruscant with Mom and Dad and our kid brother does sound kind of nice."

"Must be a sign of maturity," Jaina teased.

"Who, *me*?" Jacen said, pretending to take offense. "Nah." Then, as if to disprove her theory, he flashed a lopsided grin that made him look like a younger version of their father, Han Solo. "Want to hear a joke?"

Jaina rolled her eyes and tucked a strand of straight brown hair behind one ear to keep it away from her face. "Don't suppose you'd take no for an answer?" Then pretending to have a brilliant idea, she snapped her fingers. "Say, why don't you go up to the cockpit and tell it to Tenel Ka instead?"

She knew full well that the young warrior woman, one of their closest friends at the Jedi academy, had never even smiled—much less laughed—at Jacen's jokes, though he tried daily to coax a chuckle from her.

"I want you to be a test audience first," he said. "Then I'll go try it on Lowie—wherever he is. He's got a pretty good sense of humor for a Wookiee."

"Shouldn't be too hard to find him," Jaina said. "The *Falcon*'s not *that* big, and you can be pretty sure he's somewhere near a computer."

"Hey, you're just trying to distract me from telling my joke," Jacen said. "You ready?"

Jaina heaved a long-suffering sisterly sigh. "All right, what's the joke?"

"Okay, how long does Uncle Luke need to sleep?"

She gave a puzzled frown. "You got me."

"One Jedi *night*!" He laughed out loud, proud of his joke.

Jaina gave a melodramatic groan. "I don't think even Lowie will laugh at that one."

Jacen looked crestfallen. "I thought it was

one of my best jokes so far. I made it up myself." Then his face brightened. "Hey, I wonder if Zekk is still hanging around back on Coruscant. *He* always laughed at my jokes."

Jaina smiled at the mention of their mischievous friend, a street urchin who had been taken in and cared for by old Peckhum, the man who brought supplies to the Jedi academy. A couple of years older than the twins, Zekk had proven to be a resourceful scamp, despite his disadvantaged life. Jaina would sit and listen to Zekk for hours as he regaled her with stories of his childhood on Ennth and how, when the colony had been devastated by a natural disaster, he had escaped on the next supply ship.

Jaina had to admire Zekk's determination. The wild dark-haired boy never did anything unless he wanted to. In fact, when the captain of the rescue ship had suggested that Zekk might be better off in an orphanage or a foster home, Zekk had jumped ship to another outbound freighter at the very next stop and stowed away on it. From then on he had traveled from planet to planet, sometimes working as a cabin boy, sometimes stowing away, until one day he had met old Peckhum, who was on his way to Coruscant. Though both were independent, somehow a friendship had formed, and they had been together ever since.

"Okay, Zekk might laugh at your joke," Jaina agreed at last. "He has a strange sense of humor."

Leaving the Jedi academy far behind on Yavin 4, Jaina and Jacen watched the viewscreen in silence as the stars stretched into starlines and the *Millennium Falcon* flew into hyperspace, taking them toward Coruscant. Toward home.

Sitting at the hologame table in the rec area, Jacen studied the board. He racked his brains for a strategy to counter Lowie's previous gambit.

"It is your turn," Tenel Ka pointed out, her voice low and matter-of-fact.

Jacen had been hoping to impress his friends by winning a game or two, but he found it hard to concentrate with Tenel Ka beside him. She crossed her bare arms over her reptile-skin tunic, watching his every move. Her reddish-gold hair, tamed into numerous braids, dangled wildly around her head and shoulders every time she spoke or shifted position.

Across the table, Jaina stood behind Lowie and conferred with the ginger-furred Wookiee in a whisper, pointing from one holographic gamepiece to another. The tiny wriggling figures on the table seemed impatient for Jacen to make his next move. A thin film of perspiration formed on his forehead and upper lip. Jacen knew he didn't stand a chance against the computer whiz—especially not while Jaina was helping Lowie.

"We'll be coming out of hyperspace in about five standard minutes," Han Solo announced from the cockpit. "You kids ready?"

"Hey, Dad, can we try some target practice?" Jacen leaped to his feet, glad for the interruption. Finally, something he was good at!

Jacen loved this game their father had devised for them. Whenever he brought them back to Coruscant in the *Millennium Falcon*, Han let the twins sit in the two gun wells. As the ship approached orbit, Jacen and Jaina scanned for floating chunks of metal and debris left over from the space battles that had raged over Coruscant years before, during the overthrow of the Empire.

"We hardly ever find enough debris for both of us to shoot at," Jaina grumbled.

"Oh yeah?" Jacen said, giving her his most challenging smile. "You're just worried because last time I hit something and you didn't. I'm *sure* we're going to find some wreckage to shoot at today. I have a *good* feeling about this." He shrugged once. "But if you're just not up to it . . ."

Jaina's eyes narrowed as she accepted his challenge. A smile tugged at one corner of her mouth. "What are we waiting for?" she said. With that, she dashed toward one of the gun wells, leaving Jacen to scramble to the other. Tenel Ka followed him, while Lowie loped after Jaina, eager to help.

Behind them, the blurry monstrous figures on the hologame table hunkered down and waited for somebody to make a move.

Jacen settled into the overlarge seat of the bottom gun well. He strapped in and leaned forward to take the laser-cannon firing controls as Tenel Ka dropped into place beside him. Her granite-gray eyes narrowed, intent on the weaponry. "Watch that screen there," Jacen said. "Help me get a target. There's plenty of debris left, but it's all pretty small."

"Even small, such wreckage could be deadly to incoming ships," Tenel Ka said.

"This is a fact," Jacen answered with a grin, echoing his friend's often-used phrase. "That's why we clear it out every chance we get." Loud explosions sounded from the other gun well as Jaina began firing her quad lasers. Jacen heard a loud Wookiee roar of encouragement.

"Hey, how did she target so fast?" he said.

"Honing in," Tenel Ka said, pointing at glowing lines on the tracking screen.

"Oh! Well, I could fire too—if I was paying attention," Jacen said. He swung the four-barreled weapon into position, then watched the targeting cross move closer and closer. Maybe it was an old shielding plate from a blown-up Star Destroyer, or an empty cargo pod dumped by a fleeing smuggler. He tracked in closer. . . .

"Stay on target," Tenel Ka said. "Stay on target . . . fire!"

Jacen reacted instantly, squeezing the firing buttons, and all four laser cannons shot focused beams that vaporized the hunk of debris. "Yahoo!" he yelled. A similar whoop of delight came from the other gun well.

"It would appear that Jaina also hit her target," Tenel Ka said.

"Don't get cocky, kids," Han shouted good-naturedly from the cockpit. His copilot Chewbacca roared agreement.

"Just making the galaxy safe for peaceful navigation, Dad," Jacen called.

"We're at a tie," Jaina said. "We need one more shot each. Please, Dad?"

"You twins are always at a tie," Han answered. "If I let you keep shooting until one of you scores and the other doesn't, we'll be circling the solar system for years. Come on back up to the cockpit. We're almost home."

• • •

As the *Millennium Falcon* settled onto a clear rooftop, Lowbacca unbuckled his crash restraints and groaned. The landing on Coruscant had been smooth, and he had enjoyed his time optimizing the *Falcon*'s computers—but he was anxious to get back into the open air. Even city air, as long as he could be high enough off the ground.

By the time Lowie reached the ship's exit ramp, Jacen and Jaina had managed to unfasten their crash webbing too. The twins sped past him down the ramp and into the waiting arms of their mother. Leia Organa Solo, the New Republic's Chief of State, stood on the landing platform with her younger son, Anakin Solo, and the golden protocol droid See-Threepio.

Lowie adjusted the miniaturized translating droid, Em Teedee, at his hip and made his way down the ramp, watching the close family scene with a certain amount of envy. Dark-haired Anakin hovered beside his two older siblings, asking occasional questions, his ice-blue eyes taking in everything. Leia, her long brown hair arranged in intricate coils, looked at all three of her children with obvious pride and affection. When Han Solo came out to join the reunion, the family erupted in another joyous burst of kisses and hugs and hair ruffling.

Lowie missed his family on Kashyyyk.

Jaina said, "Thanks for letting us bring our friends home with us for the visit, Mom."

"Your friends are always welcome here," their mother replied. She stepped forward to greet Lowie with a warm smile, then bowed briefly to Tenel Ka, who had followed him down the ramp. "We're very honored to have you all here. Please, treat the palace as if it were your own home."

Though Lowie didn't say a word, Em Teedee spoke up at his waist, chiming in with a delighted voice. "Ah, See-Threepio! My counterpart, my predecessor, my . . . *mentor*! I have many things to upload to you. You'll be most distressed to hear about some of the adventures I've had since Chewbacca first delivered me to the Jedi academy—"

"To be sure! A pleasure to see you again, Em Teedee," Threepio said. "I doubt, however, that your tribulations are anything compared to the heavy diplomatic responsibilities *I* have to bear here on Coruscant. You simply couldn't believe how easily offended some of these outworld ambassadors can be!"

As the two droids chattered along in near-identical voices, Lowie rolled his large Wookiee eyes. Chewbacca, having finished the *Falcon*'s shutdown procedures, came out to join his nephew just as Lowie handed Em Teedee over to See-Threepio so that the two could reminisce as "family" for a while.

Lowie heaved a small sigh, thinking of his homeworld of Kashyyyk, his parents, and his younger sister. His uncle placed a sympathetic hand on his hairy shoulder. Perhaps Chewbacca sensed Lowie's homesickness, because he immediately launched into a description in Wookiee language of the room he had picked for his nephew to sleep in—one of the highest rooms in the Imperial Palace. Though Lowie would see no treetops from his window, Chewbacca assured him that the heights were indeed breathtaking, which should make him feel comfortable and secure. Chewie had also seen to it that the room was furnished with trees and hammocks and lush green jungle plants.

It wasn't as good as visiting home, Chewbacca said, but it was a great place for a vacation.

Tenel Ka stared at the opulent room chosen for her by Leia Organa Solo. The furniture was beautifully carved, and the draperies and bed coverings were of the finest quality. The mattress looked soft and luxurious.

It felt like home in the Fountain Palace on Hapes. Tenel Ka shuddered. She was a princess of Hapes, since her father, the son of the former queen, a powerful matriarch, now ruled the Hapes cluster with his Dathomiran wife. But Tenel Ka had kept this fact hidden from her friends at the Jedi academy, preferring instead to follow her mother's heritage from wild Dathomir. This palace was a bit *too* much like home on the Hapes central world—and Tenel Ka was uncomfortable with such amenities right now.

"Ah," she said. "Aha."

Striding to the bed, she yanked the covers off and pulled the pad onto the polished stone floor. She squatted down on it and nodded with satisfaction. The room no longer seemed as posh and fluffy—therefore, it was much more comfortable, not to mention much more suitable for a tough warrior woman. This was a fact.

2

AS SHE TRIED to sleep, Jaina thought of how different Coruscant was from the thick jungles of Yavin 4. The planet-wide capital city bustled with an intensity and energy that filtered into every aspect of daily life. Unlike the tiny moon, which managed to still itself in the quiet hours before dawn, the New Republic's central world stayed awake all the time.

Her brother Jacen blinked his bleary brown eyes as he joined her in the dining area the next morning. Tenel Ka and Lowbacca had risen early and, already at work on their morning meals, greeted the twins as they arrived. The golden protocol droid See-Threepio hurried about, making sure the guests had a fine eating experience.

Lowie ate steaming pieces of heated (but still raw) red meat from a gold-etched plate frilled with sculptured loops; Threepio had used the

best diplomatic tableware and the choicest gar-
nishes. The Wookiee youth, however, seemed to
have trouble avoiding the decorative sprigs and
delicate flowers that adorned the bloody meal.
Tenel Ka, using a small dagger to poke at her
plate, speared a piece of fruit.

"Ah, good morning, Mistress Jaina, Master
Jacen," Threepio said. "Such a pleasure to have
you home with us again."

Jaina glanced at the holographic window that
stretched across the wall of the room—actually
an image transmitted from one of the towers
elsewhere in the great city. Because their mother
was the important Chief of State, their family
quarters were protected deep within the palace,
without any real windows to the outside. Jaina
knew that many other diplomats around the city
were looking out their own false windows at the
same projected image.

"Thanks, Threepio," Jacen said. "We've been
looking forward to this vacation. Uncle Luke
has been teaching us some terrific Jedi skills,
but it can be exhausting."

The droid tapped his gold-plated hands together. "I am delighted to hear it, Master Jacen.
Although I am naturally quite busy tutoring
young Master Anakin, I have taken the liberty
of setting up a fine curriculum of studies for
you while you remain here on Coruscant. Your

guests are more than welcome to attend classes as well. Oh, it will be just like old times!"

"Classes!" Jacen interrupted as he plopped down in a chair and began to shovel breakfast into his mouth. "You're joking, right?"

"Oh, no, Master Jacen," Threepio said sternly. "You mustn't neglect your studies."

"Sorry, Threepio," Jaina said, "but we have other plans today."

Before the droid could advance his argument any further, the twins' mother came into the room. "Good morning, kids," Leia said.

Jaina smiled at her mother. Princess Leia looked as beautiful as in the old picture Jaina had seen from the Rebellion. Since that time, Leia had taken on extremely heavy political duties and devoted most of her waking hours—along with quite a few of those she should have spent sleeping—to untangling knots in the threads of diplomacy.

"What are you doing today, Mom?" Jaina asked.

Leia sighed and rolled her dark brown eyes in an expression that Jaina often unconsciously imitated. "I have a meeting with the Howler Tree People of Bendone . . . they speak a very strange language and need a team of translators. It'll take me all morning long just to hold a conversation." She closed her eyes and rubbed her fingertips at her temples. "And their ultrasonic voices give me a headache!" Leia drew a deep breath and forced a smile. "But it's part of the job. We have to keep the New Republic strong. There are always threats from the outside."

"This is a fact," Tenel Ka said gruffly. "We have seen the threat of the Shadow Academy and the Second Imperium firsthand." Lowbacca growled, clearly remembering the dark and difficult time he and the twins had experienced aboard the cloaked Imperial training station.

"Hey, I've got something that'll cheer you up, Mom," Jacen said, reaching into his pocket. "A present I kept for you."

He held out the glittering corusca gem he had snagged while using Lando Calrissian's gem-mining machinery deep in the stormy atmosphere of the gas-giant Yavin.

Leia looked down at it, blinking in amazement. "Jacen, that's a corusca gem! Is this the one you found at GemDiver Station?"

He shrugged and looked pleased. "Yeah—and I used it to cut my way free from my cell in the Shadow Academy. Would you like to have it?"

Leia's expression showed how deeply moved she was, but she closed her son's fingers around the valuable gem. "Just having you offer it to me is a very special gift," she said. "But I don't really need any more jewels or treasures. I'd like you to keep it—find a special use for it. I'm sure you'll think of something."

Jacen flushed with embarrassment, then turned an even deeper red when she gave him a big hug.

Han Solo came into the cozy dining area from the family's living quarters, freshly washed and wide awake. "So kids, what's up for you today?"

Jaina ran to give her father a hug. "Hi, Dad! We're going to spend some time catching up with our friend Zekk."

"That scruffy-looking teenaged junk hunter?" Han asked with a faint smile.

"He's *not* scruffy-looking!" Jaina said defensively.

"Hey, just kidding," Han said.

"Just make sure you don't get into trouble," Leia said.

"Trouble?" Jacen said, blinking his eyes in feigned innocence. "Us?"

Leia nodded. "Keep in mind that we're having a special diplomatic banquet tomorrow night. I don't want to have you stuck with a medical droid because of a sprained ankle—or worse."

Threepio interrupted as he tried to herd dark-haired Anakin off to a quiet room. "I do wish you'd let me keep them here to continue their studies, Mistress Leia. It would be ever so much safer." Anakin looked dejected that he couldn't go out on an adventure with his older brother and sister.

Em Teedee spoke up from Lowbacca's waist. "Well, you need have no fear for their safety, my conscientious colleague. I shall personally see to it that they behave with the utmost caution. You can count on me."

Lowbacca growled a comment, and Jaina didn't think the Wookiee was agreeing with the little translator droid.

In the open air Jaina waited next to Lowbacca, Tenel Ka, and Jacen as they stood in one of Coruscant's busy tourism information centers, a deck that jutted from the grandiose pyramid-shaped palace. Dignitaries and sightseers from across the galaxy came to the capital world to spend their credits visiting parks, museums, odd sculptures, and structures erected by ancient alien artisans.

A boxy brochure droid floated along on its repulsorlifts, babbling in an enthusiastic mechanical voice. It cheerfully listed the most wonderful sights to see, recommended eating establishments catering to various biochemistries, and gave instructions on how to arrange tours for all body types, atmosphere requirements, and languages.

Jaina fidgeted as she studied the bustling crowd—white-robed ambassadors, busy droids, and exotic creatures leashed to other strange creatures. She couldn't tell which were the masters and which the pets.

"So where is he?" Jacen said, putting his hands on his hips. His hair was tousled and his face flushed as he scanned the crowd for a familiar face.

The four young Jedi Knights stood under a sculpture of a gargoyle that broadcast shuttle arrival times from a speaker mounted in its stone mouth. Gazing up at the cloud-frothed sky, Jaina watched the silvery shapes of shuttles descending from orbit. She tried to amuse herself by identifying the vehicle types as they passed, but all the while she wondered what had delayed their friend Zekk. She checked her chronometer again and saw he was only about two standard minutes late. She was just anxious to see him.

Suddenly, a figure dropped directly in front of her from the gargoyle statue overhead—a wiry youth with shoulder-length hair one shade lighter than black. He wore a broad grin on his narrow face, and his sparkling green eyes, wide with delight, showed a darker corona surrounding the emerald irises. "Hi, guys!"

Jaina gasped, but Tenel Ka reacted with dizzying speed. In the fraction of a second following Zekk's landing, the warrior girl whipped out her fibercord rope and snapped a lasso around him, pulling the strand tight.

"Hey!" the boy cried. "Is this the way Jedi Knights greet people?"

Jacen laughed and slapped Tenel Ka on the back. "Good one!" he said. "Tenel Ka, meet our friend Zekk."

Tenel Ka blinked once. "It is a pleasure."

The wiry boy struggled against the restraining cords. "Likewise," he said sheepishly. "Now, if you wouldn't mind untying me?"

Tenel Ka flicked her wrist to release the fibercord.

While Zekk indignantly brushed himself off, Jaina introduced their Wookiee friend Lowbacca. Jaina grinned as she watched Zekk. Though the older boy had a slight build, he was tough as blaster-proof armor. Under the smudges of dirt and grime on his cheeks, she thought, he was probably rather nice-looking—but then, *she* wasn't one to talk about smudges on the face, was she?

Recovering himself, Zekk raised his eyebrows and flashed a roguish smile. "I've been waiting for you guys," he said. "We've got plenty of stuff to see and do . . . and I need your help to salvage something."

"Where are we headed?" Jacen asked.

Zekk grinned. "Someplace we're not supposed to go—of course."

Jaina laughed. "Well then, what are we waiting for?"

Jacen looked out at the sprawling city and thought of all the places he had yet to explore.

Coruscant had been the government world not only of the New Republic, but also of the Empire, and of the Old Republic before that. Skyscrapers covered virtually every open space, built higher and higher as the centuries passed and new governments moved in. The tallest buildings were kilometers high. Many had been destroyed during the bloody battles of the Rebellion and had recently been rebuilt by huge construction droids. Other parts of the planet-wide city remained a jumble of decay and wreckage, their abandoned lower levels and piled garbage forgotten over the years.

The buildings were so high that the gaps between them formed sheer canyons that vanished to a point in the dark depths where sunlight never penetrated. Catwalks and pedestrian tubes linked the buildings, weaving them together into a giant maze. The lower forty or fifty floors were generally restricted from normal traffic; only refugees and daring big-game hunters in search of monstrous urban scavenger beasts were willing to risk venturing into the shadowy underworld.

Like a native guide, Zekk led the four friends down connecting elevators, slide tubes, and rusty metal stairs, and across the catwalks from one building to another. Jacen followed, exhilarated. He wasn't sure he knew exactly where they were anymore, but he loved to explore new places, never knowing what sort of interesting plants or creatures he might find.

The skyscraper walls rose like glass-and-metal cliff faces, with only a narrow wedge of daylight shining from above. As Zekk took the companions farther down, the buildings seemed broader, the walls rougher. Mushy blobs of fungus grew from cracks in the massive construction blocks; fringed lichens, some glowing with phosphorescent light, caked the walls. Lowbacca looked decidedly uneasy, and Jacen remembered that the lanky Wookiee had grown up on Kashyyyk, where the deep forest underworld was an extremely dangerous place.

High overhead Jacen could hear the cries of sleek winged creatures—predatory hawk-bats that lived in the city on Coruscant. The breeze picked up, carrying with it heavy, warm scents of rotting garbage from far below. His stomach grew queasy, but he pressed on. Zekk didn't seem to notice. Tenel Ka, Lowie, and Jaina hurried behind them.

They proceeded across a roofed-in walkway where many of the transparisteel ceiling panels had been smashed out, leaving only a wire reinforcement mesh that whistled in the breezes. Jacen noted etched symbols along the walls, all of them vaguely threatening. Some reminded Jacen of curved knives and fanged mouths, but the most common design showed a sharp triangle surrounding a targeting cross. It looked to Jacen like the tip of an arrow heading straight between his eyes.

"Hey, Zekk, what's that design?" He pointed to the triangular symbol.

Frowning, Zekk glanced around them in all directions and then whispered, "It means we have to be very quiet down here and move as fast as we can. We don't want to go into any of these buildings."

"But why not?" Jacen asked.

"The Lost Ones," Zekk said. "It's a gang. They live down here—kids who ran away from home or were abandoned by their parents because they were so much trouble. Nasty types, mostly."

"Let's hope they stay lost," Jaina said.

Zekk glanced up, his forehead creased with troubled thoughts. "The Lost Ones might even be looking at us right now, but they've never managed to catch me yet," he said. "It's like a game between us."

"How have you managed to get away from them all the time?" Jaina whispered.

"I'm just good at it. Like I'm a good scavenger," Zekk answered, sounding cocky. "I may not be in training as a Jedi Knight, but I make do with what skills I've got. Just streetwise, I guess. But," he continued, "even though I have kind of an . . . understanding with them, I'd rather not push it. Especially not while I'm with the twin children of the Chief of State."

"This is a fact," Tenel Ka said grimly. She kept her hands close to her utility belt in case she needed to draw a weapon.

Zekk quickly ushered them through dilapidated corridors that were heavily decorated with the gang symbols. Jacen saw signs of recent habitation, wrappers from prepackaged food, bright metallic spots where salvaged equipment had been torn away from its housings.

At last they moved on to deeper levels. They all breathed more easily, although Zekk confessed even he had not fully explored this far down. "I think it's a shortcut," he said. "I need your help so I can recover something very valuable." He raised his dark eyebrows. "I think you'll like it—particularly you, Jacen."

Zekk made his living by scavenging: salvaging lost equipment, removing scraps of precious metal from abandoned dwellings. He found lost treasures to sell to inventors, spare parts to repair obsolete machines, trinkets that could be turned into souvenirs. He seemed to have a real skill for finding items that other scavengers had missed over the centuries, somehow knowing where to look, sometimes in the unlikeliest of places.

They descended an outer staircase, slick with damp moss from moisture trickling down the walls. Jacen had to squint just to see the steps. As they turned the corner of the building, Zekk stopped in surprise. In the dim light reflected from far above, Jacen could see a strange jumble protruding from the side of the building— smashed construction bricks, naked durasteel girders . . . and a crashed transport shuttle. From the drooping algae and fungus growing on its outer hull, the damaged shuttle appeared to have been there a long time.

"Wow!" Zekk said. "I didn't even know this was here." He hurried forward, edging his way along the damaged walkway. "I don't believe it. The salvage hasn't even been picked over. See— I'm lucky again!"

"That's an Old Republic craft," Jaina said. "At least seventy years old. They haven't used those in . . . I can't even remember. What a find!"

Tenel Ka and Lowie held the creaking ship steady as Zekk scrambled inside to look around. He poked into storage compartments, looking for valuables. "Plenty of components are still intact. Engine still looks good," he called. "Whoa, and here's the driver. I guess his parking permit ran out."

Jacen came up behind him to see a tattered skeleton strapped into the cockpit.

"Oh, do be careful," Em Teedee said from Lowbacca's waist. "Abandoned vehicles can be terribly dangerous—and you might get dirty as well."

"Was this what you wished to show us, Zekk?" Tenel Ka said.

The older boy stood, bumping his head on a bent girder that ran along the shuttle's ceiling. "No, no, this is a new discovery. I'll have to spend a lot more time down here." He grinned. Engine grease smudged his face, and his hands were grimy from digging through compartments. "I can get this stuff later. I need your help for something different. Let's go."

Zekk scrambled out of the shuttle wreckage and grasped the rusted handrail on the rickety walkway. He looked around to get his bearings, making certain he wouldn't forget the location of this prize. The skull of the unlucky pilot stared out at them through empty eye sockets.

"Looks like you really do know this place like the back of your hand," Jacen commented as Zekk led them elsewhere.

"I've had plenty of practice," Zekk said. "*Some* of us don't take regular trips off planet and go to diplomatic functions all the time. I have to amuse myself with what I can find."

It was midmorning by the time they reached Zekk's destination. The dark-haired boy rubbed his hands together in anticipation, and pointed far below. "Down there—can you see it?"

Jacen looked down, *down* over a ledge to see a rusted construction crawler latched to a wall about ten meters away . . . completely out of reach. The construction crawler was a crane-like mechanical apparatus that had once ridden tracks along the side of the building, scouring the walls clean, effecting repairs, applying duracrete sealant—but this contraption had frozen up and begun to decay at least a century ago. Its interlinked rusted braces were clogged with fuzzy growths of moss and fungus.

Jacen squinted again, wondering why the other boy meant to salvage parts from such an old machine—but then he saw the bushy mass, a tangle of uprooted wires and cables woven together, bristling with insulation material, torn strips of cloth, and plastic. It looked almost like a . . .

"It's a hawk-bat's nest," Zekk said. "Four eggs inside. I can see them from here, but I can't get down there by myself. If I can snatch even one of those eggs, I could sell it for enough credits to live on for a month."

"And you want *us* to help you get it?" Jaina asked.

"That's the idea," Zekk said. "Your friend Tenel Ka there has a pretty strong rope—as I found out! And some of you look like good climbers, especially that Wookiee."

Em Teedee shrilled, "Oh no, Lowbacca. You simply can*not* climb down there! I absolutely forbid it." Lowie hadn't looked too eager at first, but the translating droid's admonishment only served to convince him otherwise. The Wookiee growled an agreement to Zekk's plan.

Tenel Ka attached her grappling hook to the side of the walkway. "I am a strong climber," she said. "This is a fact."

Zekk rubbed his hands together with delight. "Excellent."

"Let me get the eggs," Jacen said, eager to touch the smooth, warm shells, to study the nest configuration. "I've always wanted to see one up close." This was such a rare opportunity. Hawk-bats were common in the deep alleyways of Coruscant, but they were horrendously difficult to capture alive.

Pulling the fibercord taut, Tenel Ka wrapped her hands around it and began lowering herself to the old construction crawler. Jacen had seen her descend the walls of the Great Temple on Yavin 4, but now he watched with renewed amazement as she walked backward down the side of the building, relying only on the strength of her supple arms and muscular legs.

Jacen admired the girl from Dathomir—but he wished he could make her laugh. He had been telling Tenel Ka his best jokes for as long as he had known her, but he still hadn't managed to coax even the smallest smile from her. She seemed not to have a sense of humor, but he would keep trying.

Tenel Ka reached the construction crawler and anchored the fibercord, gesturing with her arm to summon him down. Jacen wrapped the cord around himself and started down the slick wall, trying to imitate Tenel Ka. He used the Force to keep his balance, nudging his feet when necessary, and soon found himself standing beside Tenel Ka on the teetering platform.

"Piece of cake," he panted, brushing his hands together.

"No thank you," Tenel Ka said. "I am not hungry."

Jacen chuckled, but he knew the warrior girl didn't even realize she had made a joke.

Lowie slid down the fibercord with ease, while Em Teedee wailed all the way. "Oh, I can't watch! I'd rather switch off my optical sensors."

When they all stood on the creaking platform, Jacen bent over, straining to reach the tangled nest just below. "I'm going to climb down there," he said. "I'll pass the eggs up."

Before anyone could argue, he dropped between two thin girders, holding a crossbar to reach the piping brace that supported the odd nest. The eggs were brown, mottled with green, camouflaged as knobs of masonry covered with pale lichen. Each was about the size of Jacen's outspread hand; when he touched the warm shells, the texture was hard and rough, like rock. With the Force, he could sense the growing baby creature inside. Perhaps he could use the Force to levitate the prize up to his friends.

He smiled, tingly with wonder as he hefted one of the eggs. It wasn't heavy at all. As he touched a second egg, though, he heard a shrill shriek from above, coming closer.

Tenel Ka shouted a warning. "Look out, Jacen!"

Jacen looked up and saw the sleek form of the mother hawk-bat, swooping down at him and screaming in fury, metallic claws extended, wings studded with spikes. The hawk-bat's wing-span was about two meters. Its head consisted mostly of a horny beak with sharp ivory teeth, ready to tear a victim to shreds.

"Uh-oh," Jacen said.

Lowie bellowed in alarm. Tenel Ka grabbed for a throwing knife—but Jacen knew he couldn't wait for help.

The creature dove toward him like a missile, and Jacen closed his eyes to reach out with the Force. His special talent had always been with animals. He could communicate with them, sense their feelings and express his own to them. "It's all right," he whispered. "I'm sorry we were invading your nest. *Calm*. It's all right. *Peace*."

The hawk-bat pulled up from her dive and clutched one of the corroded lower crossbars with durasteel-hard claws. Jacen could hear the squeaking sound as the claws scraped rust off the metal, but he maintained his calm.

"We didn't mean to hurt your babies," he said. "We won't take them all. I need only one, and I promise you it'll be delivered to a fine and safe place . . . a beautiful zoo where it will be raised and cared for and admired by millions of people from across the galaxy."

The hawk-bat hissed and pushed her hard

beak closer to Jacen, blowing foul breath from between sharp teeth. He knew the hawk-bat was extremely skeptical, but Jacen projected images of a bright aviary, a place where the young hawk-bat would be fed delicacies all its life, where it could fly freely, yet never need to fear other predators or starvation . . . or being shot at by gang members. Jacen snatched the last vision—blurred figures of young humans shooting as she hunted between tall buildings—from the mother's mind.

This last fear convinced the mother, and she flapped her spiked leathery wings, backing away from the nest and leaving Jacen safe . . . for the moment. He grinned up at his friends.

Tenel Ka stood poised, dagger in hand, ready to jump down and fight. Jacen felt a pleasant warm glow to think that she was willing to defend him. He took the hawk-bat egg he was holding and used the Force to carefully levitate it into Jaina's hands. She cradled it, then handed it to Zekk.

"What did you do?" Zekk called.

"I made a deal with the hawk-bat," he said. "Let's go."

"But what about those other eggs?" Zekk said, holding his treasure with great amazement.

"You only get one," Jacen answered. "That

was the deal. Now we'd better get out of here—
and hurry." He scrambled up to join Lowie and
Tenel Ka.

Lowie climbed the fibercord first, racing up
the side of the building to the upper ledge.
Jacen urged the others to greater speed, and
finally, when they were all standing back on the
walkway, Zekk said, "I thought you made a deal
with the mother. Why do we have to hurry?"

Jacen continued to hustle them out of sight of
the construction crawler. "Because hawk-bats
have extremely short memories."

3

AS THE FIVE companions left the hawk-bat's nest behind, Jaina stuck close to Zekk. She watched the dark-haired boy move instinctively, hurrying through the maze of upper and lower walkways and cross-connecting bridges as he made a beeline back to his living quarters. The green-eyed boy beamed with self-congratulatory pride at the precious egg he held, as if it were a trophy he had hoped to win for a long time.

"Peckhum is going to be so pleased!" Zekk crowed, looking from Jaina to Jacen. "He'll know just what to do with it. He's got a line on everyone who's looking for anything." He glanced sidelong at Jacen again. "Don't worry about it. We'll find a good home for this baby, just like you promised, Jacen. It shouldn't be too hard for a professional zoologist to incubate this egg until it hatches."

Tenel Ka cleared her throat and said ominously, "*If* we bring the egg back intact."

Jaina suddenly noticed that they had returned to the abandoned levels emblazoned with gang graffiti. *The Lost Ones.*

The sharp corners of the cross in a triangle symbol seemed brighter now, as if freshly painted. Jaina wondered if the gang members could have marked their territory afresh in the short time since the young Jedi Knights had passed through. If the gang members kept such a careful eye out for everything, they might have spotted the five companions already.

Maybe they were watching from hidden, shadowy corners right now. . . .

Tenel Ka tensed and pulled out a small throwing knife, looking from side to side. She seemed alert, ready to spring at the first sign of danger, but Jaina didn't feel safe. With her Jedi senses, she felt a tingle down her spine.

"If the Lost Ones are so tough and powerful, how come we've never heard of them before?" Jacen looked around nervously in the creaking, musty buildings.

"Because you never come down here," Zekk answered. "Whenever we get together, you either have me come to the Imperial Palace or we meet in the safe upper levels. I'll bet your parents would blow their thrusters if they knew where we were right now."

"We can take care of ourselves," Tenel Ka said defensively, flashing her tiny dagger.

"Dear me, I shouldn't be so certain about that, if I were you," Em Teedee replied from Lowie's waist. The young Wookiee groaned.

Zekk smiled thinly. "Down here you can see how *I* live every day. I don't have anyone to wash my hands for me or cook my meals, you know. And I don't have the luxury of worrying about how to amuse myself. Every day is a search—I'm just lucky I have a special knack for finding things."

Jaina was surprised to hear a hint of resentment behind her friend's words. "Zekk, if you needed anything, you should have just asked. We could have found you new quarters, given you credits to spend—"

"Who said I wanted that?" he responded through clenched teeth. "I don't need charity. I've got my freedom here. I can do whatever I want. Besides, it's more satisfying to live by my own wits than to be pampered and coddled all the time."

Em Teedee piped up, "Well really, Master Zekk! It might interest you to learn that not *everyone* minds being pampered and coddled." Jaina ignored the translating droid and wondered if Zekk really meant what he said.

"Nothing personal," Zekk said with shrug. He

looked up at the cross-in-triangle symbol. "Being a gang member doesn't impress me either. Their leader Norys—who's our age—is a big bully who likes to throw his weight around. I can run my way through the lower levels better than any of the Lost Ones, so he's been after me to join for a long time. He'd love to have me as his right-hand man, but I'm too independent for that. I work for myself."

They stood at the entrance to a sheer-walled building, near one end of a dilapidated covered walkway that extended to an adjacent sky-scraper. More threatening gang symbols marked the inside walls. Half of the windows were broken, and confined breezes whispered through the walkway like voices warning them to go back.

Zekk looked behind him. "This building we're in is the headquarters of the Lost Ones. We're taking a pretty big risk being here." His emerald eyes sparkled. "Kind of exciting, isn't it?"

The building was large and dark, filled with cavernous spaces of empty meeting chambers, offices, and abandoned supply rooms. Jaina wondered if any record or blueprint of this ancient building still existed in the vast computer archives of the Imperial Information Center.

"I don't think you have to worry about Norys,

though," Zekk said, raising his voice. "He talks big, but his ambitions are definitely low. He has no interest in becoming anything more than the biggest bully in a run-down section of a single building on an average planet in a big galaxy." Zekk's voice sounded taunting. "He'll never go anywhere, because his dreams are small."

Just then ceiling panels smashed down from above them, and a dozen wiry young men and women dropped to the floor. They looked scuffed and dirty, with hard, lean faces; each held an interesting cobbled-together weapon scavenged from sharp pieces of scrap.

"You trying to annoy me, trash collector?" the biggest burly young man said. His face was broad and dark, his eyes close-set, his teeth crooked as he ground his jaws together and spread his lips in a sneer.

"It's not polite to eavesdrop, Norys," Zekk said.

Then the gang leader's eyes fixed on the precious hawk-bat egg that Zekk cradled close to his chest. "What has the little trash collector found?" Norys said. "Hey, everybody! Looks like we're gonna have fresh eggs for morning meal."

Lowbacca growled loudly enough to startle the Lost Ones, baring his long Wookiee fangs. Zekk looked suddenly nervous, as if the valuable hawk-bat egg made him vulnerable in new ways.

"What do you want the egg for?" Jacen said.

"He only wants it because *I* want it," Zekk said. "He'll probably smash it, not knowing what it's worth."

Tenel Ka now held a throwing dagger at the ready in each hand. The Lost Ones looked at her and Lowie, then at the three seemingly easier targets of Zekk and the twins.

"In a case like this," Zekk said, moving slowly, extending the mottled egg gradually, as if reluctant to surrender it to the brawny gang member, "the most sensible idea is to . . . *run!*"

He whirled and dashed onto the rickety walkway. The vibration of his running knocked loose a broken wall plate, which dropped silently into the murky depths below. The young Jedi Knights reacted quickly and scrambled after their friend onto the covered bridge.

The gang members howled and gave pursuit, clattering their crude weapons against the walls.

Out in the middle of the dilapidated walkway Zekk suddenly pulled to a stop as a gang member—an angry young woman who looked even tougher than Tenel Ka—appeared from the opposite building and stood ominously at the far entrance.

"We're trapped," Jaina said with a hard gulp. This did not seem like a good place for a standoff.

Zekk looked back and forth, as if seeking inspiration in the middle of the swaying bridge. The cold wind sighed through the broken windows and gaps in the flooring. "Just to be fair," he said, crossing his arms with feigned good humor, "I'll let you guys solve this one. Got any ideas?"

Jaina tried to think of something she could do with what Uncle Luke had taught them at the Jedi academy. With uninterrupted concentration she could manipulate objects with the Force, but she couldn't think of any way her fledgling powers could help them escape.

Norys strode forward, his chest puffed with confidence. "Now give me that egg, trash collector, and maybe we won't throw you over the edge!"

Just then a screeching sound came from above, a blood-curdling animal shriek. A predator's heavy shadow swept like a dark blanket over the cracked windows of the walkway.

With another loud scream, the mother hawk-bat struck the side windows, smashing against the wire mesh that barely held the frames in place. She spat and hissed, her sharp beak ripping at the wires, her forked tongue thrashing as she dug her claws in, trying to get at Norys. The gang leader staggered backward with a surprised yelp.

Zekk protected the egg again, holding it to his chest. At the same time, Lowie—focusing on the lone woman guarding the opposite end of the walkway—let out a ferocious roar and charged forward.

"Oh, my!" Em Teedee squeaked. "Would anyone object if I switched off my optical sensors again so I don't have to watch?"

Distracted by the attacking hawk-bat and startled by the snarling battering ram of Wookiee fur, the gang member backed off and leaped aside.

"Well, what are we waiting for?" Jaina cried. Zekk ducked low to protect the hawk-bat egg as he ran after her. Jacen followed them, while Tenel Ka turned once to threaten the Lost Ones with her throwing daggers before bringing up the rear, sprinting along on her muscular legs.

Seeing them escape, the mother hawk-bat shrieked one more time, then flew off, as if satisfied.

Zekk kept running while Norys yelled after them. "We'll catch you next time, trash collector. Do you hear me?" he shouted. "You'll join our gang—one way or another."

Zekk didn't respond as he led the young Jedi

Knights through a maze of stairwells, slides, and lifts in the lower levels, climbing up to rickety catwalks, then higher to lighted levels. He was panting, but his flushed face wore a grin of exhilaration. Triumphant, Zekk cradled the hawk-bat egg close to his body.

"I thought you said hawk-bats had short-term memories," he gasped.

Jacen shrugged and looked sheepish. "Aren't you glad I was wrong?"

"Yes," Jaina said. "We all are."

"Come on," Zekk said. "Let's get this egg back home."

4

VORACIOUSLY HUNGRY AFTER their adventure, the four young Jedi Knights followed Zekk back to where he made his home. Since much of Coruscant's population had fled the capital world during the devastating battles of the Rebellion, many of the midlevel apartments had been left empty but still serviceable. People scraped out a decent existence there without being forced to live in squalor far below at the bottom levels.

For years, Zekk had shared quarters with old Peckhum. The thin, gray-haired man had no particular career, but spent his days doing odd jobs such as transporting cargo in his battered ship, the *Lightning Rod*, or performing whatever duties the New Republic required. Zekk and the old supply runner got along well and helped each other as if they were family, providing mutual support, company, and a place to stay.

Zekk led the companions through dim corridors on the way to his apartment. At the entrance Jaina saw that Peckhum had installed a new messaging center beside the door so that visitors could leave videonotes if no one was home.

"We can kick back here for a while," Zekk said, tucking the hawk-bat egg into the crook of his elbow as his nimble fingers punched in an access code.

The metal door slid aside to reveal a paradise of junk—rooms stacked high with salvaged items, partially restored antiques, and strange gadgets whose original use had long since been forgotten. A small sapphire-feathered bird flitted around inside, but Jaina couldn't tell if the creature was a pet or just some stray that had wandered in to look for nesting materials.

A grizzled old man stood up from a rickety table where he had been poring over manifest files on a scuffed datapad. He had lank gray hair, a leathery face, and a broad smile—and he very much needed a shave. "Ah, Zekk, you're back." He looked past the teenager. "And you've brought guests. Hello, my young Jedi friends."

Zekk sealed the door behind them, and Jacen immediately began trying to catch the bird, while Tenel Ka poked around suspiciously in the stacked cases and gadgets, as if attempting to uncover traps. Lowie sniffed at a cluttered jumble of electronic equipment.

Zekk beamed proudly as he held out the mottled hawk-bat egg. "Look at this prize!" he said. "How much do you think we can get for it?"

Peckhum nodded with enthusiasm as he held out his hands to take the egg gently in his grasp. "More than a hundred credits, I'd guess. Plenty of zoos and biological establishments are begging for a specimen like this."

Jacen said sternly, "Just make sure it goes to a good home. I made promises to its mother."

Peckhum laughed, shaking his head. "I'll never understand you Jedi Knights. But I don't suppose that'll be too difficult," he said. "In fact, I think I'll even talk to your mother—I heard a rumor that the Chief of State was looking for some unusual zoological specimens."

Jacen blinked his eyes in astonishment. "*Our* mom wanted to collect weird animals? She could have just asked me. . . ."

Peckhum shrugged. "I didn't ask *why* she wanted it. I think it's for some sort of diplomatic gift. And I think this egg, with the proper incubating apparatus, might just do the trick!"

Jaina found a place to sit down, perching herself on a stack of recycled blankets that

Peckhum no doubt intended to sell to some alien merchant. Zekk hurried off to prepare a quick lunch. "Last time we saw you, Peckhum," Jaina said conversationally, "you were cornered by a jungle monster on Yavin 4."

Peckhum laughed nervously at the memory. "I haven't been that scared in a dozen years!" he said. "Let's hope your jungle moon gets a little more civilized."

"Are you making another supply run to the Jedi academy soon?" Jacen asked.

"No, I've been assigned to riding the mirrors up in Coruscant orbit," Peckhum said. "It's a lonely job, but the pay is good—and somebody's got to do it. Besides, it's relaxing . . . if you look at it that way."

Because so much of the surface of Coruscant was covered by cities, engineers had long ago found ways to make even the cold northern and southern latitudes more habitable. By focusing sunlight from huge orbiting mirrors, they could direct enough warmth to thaw land as far north as the arctic, so that millions upon millions could live even in Coruscant's less hospitable areas.

Jaina understood the engineering difficulties of operating the huge automated mirrors, of making sure that the beams of directed sunlight shone down on appropriate areas. The job was not unlike the ancient task of running a lighthouse on an ocean world, where people worked alone, ready for emergencies that rarely came.

"Such an austere assignment would provide a good environment for contemplation," Tenel Ka pointed out.

"It does that, all right," Peckhum said. "I just wish conditions weren't so . . . basic."

"What makes the mirror station so uncomfortable?" Jaina asked. "Don't you have entertainment systems and food-processing units up there?"

Peckhum snorted. "According to the design, yes. But they're all malfunctioning. The mirror stations were set up long ago, even before the Emperor took over. During the Imperial years, riding the mirror station was a punishment assigned to stormtroopers who had disobeyed orders.

"Nowadays, the food-prep units, entertainment systems, temperature control systems— even the communication systems—all fritz out randomly. No repair tech is willing to go up and give the whole station an overhaul. The New Republic has so much other business that I'm afraid getting spiffy holovideo reception for the mirror station just isn't high on anyone's priority list."

Jaina pursed her lips and placed her chin in

her hands. "Those symptoms you described sound familiar," she said. "Could be you need a new central multitasking unit. That might fix everything all at once."

Peckhum switched off his datapad and tucked it into a satchel hanging from the seat. "Don't I know it! But those units are expensive and hard to come by. I've requested a new system five times, and it's always been turned down. 'The resources of the New Republic are allocated according to greatest need,'" he said, as if quoting from a report. "My comfort isn't a great enough need." He scratched his stubbled chin. "Oh well, I'll survive. It's a job. Last month I used some of my own credits to get a hand-held holoplayer to take up with me. It'll do."

Zekk came out of the kitchen area balancing a stack of self-heating ration cans in his arms. "I know where we can get a central multitasking unit!" He pressed his chin against the top can in the stack to hold them all in position. "Remember that old shuttle we found? Models like that had lots of subsystems. They must have had units to run everything."

"Sure did," Jaina said, nodding vigorously. "Those outdated passenger shuttles all had central multitasking units. They were cumbersome, but they worked."

Peckhum grinned, then frowned. "Well, I'm

leaving tomorrow morning, and I'm not sure how I'd install one of those units myself, even if you did get it."

Zekk waved his hand in dismissal. "Relax, Peckhum—I'll get one for you by the time you return. I promise."

Jaina piped up, seeing an opportunity. "And maybe next time you go up to the mirror station, we could go along and help install it." Lowbacca bellowed his interest in the project as well.

Peckhum's eyes widened with surprised delight. "Well, I suppose that might work after all. Let's celebrate by eating lunch."

The old man swept unsorted debris from a low table, clearing a spot for Zekk to set down the stacked cans of food. The dark-haired boy studied them and passed out rations to everyone. Warm steam curled up from open lids as thermal units heated the contents.

Jaina sniffed at hers suspiciously, and Jacen poked into the goo, while Tenel Ka studied the label seriously. Lowie gave a doubtful growl.

"You needn't complain, Master Lowbacca," Em Teedee said. "I'm certain it's quite nutritious. See? The label bears the Imperial stamp of approval."

Zekk held up one of the cans. "These are old stormtrooper rations. We found an entire cache in one of the lower buildings. They don't taste like much, but they have all our nutritional requirements."

Tenel Ka dug in, grunting with satisfaction. "Quite acceptable," she said.

Jaina stirred the grayish puttylike substance, smiled as Zekk dug in, then took a small bite herself. It didn't taste bad. In fact, it didn't taste like *anything*, so she ate courteously. When they had finished, She stood up, meeting Zekk's emerald-green gaze. "Want to join *us* for a meal next time?"

Zekk brightened. "Fine with me. When?"

"Well," Jaina said, biting her lower lip and considering, "since Peckhum is leaving you all alone, why don't you come to the Imperial Palace tomorrow night? We're taking a holiday with my parents in the morning, but we're having some sort of special banquet in the evening. Banquets are usually pretty boring, but I'm sure we could get you invited."

"Really?" Zekk said.

"Sure," Jaina answered.

"That's right," Jacen agreed. "We'll probably give Threepio the time of his life tending to us."

5

FAT SNOWFLAKES FELL in skirling patterns of white against white. There was ice and snow as far as the eye could see on the frozen mountains of Coruscant's polar ice caps. Jaina's exhaled breath produced small puffs of fog in front of her face. Her nose and throat tingled with cold as she inhaled, reveling in the feeling. The crisp air was fresh and clean and delicious.

The tauntaun beneath her, however, smelled *bad*. The creature was supposed to be well behaved, but Jaina didn't think the Bothan stable manager at the polar corrals spent any more time training the wild arctic animals than he did bathing them.

The tauntaun was a white-furred reptile with curved horns jutting from its head. It ran on muscular three-toed hind legs designed to crunch across the snow at high speed. The animals were native to the ice world of Hoth, where the

Rebel Alliance had long ago established a secret base. In recent years, though, an enterprising stable manager had transported a few of the beasts to Coruscant's ice caps, intending to offer tauntaun riding as an activity for winter-sports enthusiasts who came to the north pole. But the tauntauns had become surly and stubborn after being transplanted from their home, and Jaina couldn't see how riding one was supposed to be fun.

Her tauntaun fought the bit in its mouth as she tried to make it keep pace with Jacen and his mount. Anakin stayed closer to their father, who hung back next to Leia. Han Solo had claimed to be an expert rider of the unco-operative tauntauns, but Jaina giggled as she watched her father experience plenty of difficulty as they raced across the snows.

The part Jaina enjoyed most was just being able to spend a few hours away from the bustling city with her family, so they could be kids and their parents could be parents—if only for a little while.

Lowie had already made plans with his uncle Chewbacca, and See-Threepio had offered to spend the day showing Tenel Ka the finest obstacle courses and training facilities that Coruscant had to offer.

Before long, she and Jacen and their friends

would have to return to the Jedi academy to continue their training, and Han and Leia would get back to their work building the New Republic.

For now, though, they were on vacation.

"Race you," Jacen called, hunching over his tauntaun.

Jaina took up the challenge instantly. "Well then, what are we waiting for?" She leaned forward and jabbed her heels into the side of the snow lizard.

But just as Jacen whooped his own challenge, his tauntaun stopped dead in its tracks and refused to go a centimeter farther.

Jaina's mount lurched forward at full speed, but she wasn't able to gloat over her victory in the race, because she had as much trouble getting her tauntaun to *stop* as Jacen had getting his to move.

"More soup?" Leia asked, huddling next to the thermal container on the snow.

Jaina shook her head. "Don't think I could eat another bite, Mom."

"Hey, I'd love some more," Jacen said.

"Me too," Anakin chimed in.

"Make that three hungry Solo men," Han Solo added with a lopsided grin, handing his soup cup to Leia. "Never could resist one of your packed lunches."

"Yeah, I can push food-prep buttons better than anyone you know," Leia said wryly.

Jaina sighed with contentment, glad just to relax. After the tauntaun riding, they had spent hours turbo-skiing, having snowball fights, and building cities in the snow. Now, seated on a thick slab of heat-reflective insulfoam, Jaina spread her arms wide, catching snowflakes on her gloved hands. "I wish we could do this more often," she said.

"Maybe we should," her mother replied.

Anakin slurped the last of his soup. "I'll be coming to the Jedi academy again soon," he said. "We can have more meals together then."

"Oh, that reminds me," Leia said. "Don't forget, I'm hosting a very important banquet tonight for the new ambassador from Karnak Alpha."

"Where's Karnak Alpha?" Jacen asked. "I don't think I've ever heard of it."

"Out beyond the Hapes Cluster near the Core Systems," his mother answered.

"Aren't there still some Imperial strongholds in the Core Systems?" asked Jaina.

"Sure are," Han Solo replied. "That's why your mother thinks this dinner is so important. You'll have to be on your best behavior."

Jacen groaned. "If it's so important, how come *we* have to be there?"

Leia smiled warmly. "I'd like you to meet the ambassador. Children play a very special part in the society of Karnak Alpha. They are seen as great treasures that grow richer every day. In Karnak society, the more children you have, the more status and honor you gain. Their government even has a children's council."

"Blaster bolts!" Jacen said. "I almost forgot. We invited Zekk over for evening meal tonight."

"Can he come to the banquet too, Mom?" Jaina asked.

Leia looked flustered, an expression Jaina did not often see on her mother's face. "Zekk? Your young friend from the streets?"

"Aren't you always saying that everyone is valuable, no matter what their background is?" Jaina put in, a little defensively.

"Yeeeesss . . . ," Leia said, drawing the word out.

"Please? If you say yes, I'll even let you braid my hair," Jaina offered hopefully. She glanced at her brothers, looking for support, and saw Anakin's face take on that peculiar measuring look it always did when he was solving a problem.

"If they value children so much, won't the ambassador be happy to have another kid join us?" Anakin said.

Leia's face cleared. "Yes, of course—that's

right. Your friend Zekk is more than welcome to come. In fact, we'll invite Lowie and Tenel Ka too."

Jaina laughed with relief. "Great! I'll let them know as soon as we get back."

Jacen finished his soup and stood up. "Do we have to leave right away?"

Han consulted his chronometer. "No, we've got an hour or two yet."

"Well, in that case," Jacen said, "I'll race you all to those hills!"

Everyone laughed and dove for their turbo-skis.

6

AT THE APPOINTED hour that evening, Zekk arrived at the enormous palace and was ushered inside. New Republic guards checked his name against the approved-visitor list and let him proceed into the elegant corridors, with their high vaulted ceilings. Although he knew his way to Jacen and Jaina's quarters, the uniformed soldiers insisted on "escorting" him, which Zekk found somewhat intimidating.

His new formal clothes were stiff and exceedingly uncomfortable, but he knew that this dinner was an important occasion. He silently vowed not to embarrass anyone. He especially didn't want to disappoint the twins.

Before old Peckhum had departed for his lonely mirror-station duties, he'd helped Zekk select a few items of formal clothing, and the young man had also gone out trading, bartering some of his best trinkets and artifacts for a particularly slick jacket. Now he felt like a dandy as he rode the turbolift up to the higher levels and wound his way through the maze of corridors to the Chief of State's quarters.

The protocol droid See-Threepio met Zekk at the doorway and hustled him inside, dismissing the soldier escort. "Ah, there you are, young Master Zekk. We must hurry—you're late! We have preparations to make."

Zekk tugged at his uncomfortable formal suit. "What do you mean 'preparations'? I'm all ready, I'm dressed . . . what more could you want?"

Threepio tsked through his mouth speaker and brushed the front of Zekk's shirt. "Dear me. These clothes are indeed fine and they are most . . . *interesting*. According to my files they were quite fashionable some decades ago. Quite an historical find, I should say."

Zekk felt a stab of disappointment. He had worked so hard, doing his absolute best to prepare for this special event—and in the space of a few seconds the prissy droid had dismissed all of his efforts.

Leia Organa Solo hurried out of the back room, her dark eyes widening as she saw him. "Oh . . . uh, hello Zekk. Glad you could make it." Her gaze seemed to dissect Zekk; he clenched his teeth and tried not to show any embarrassment, though he was sure his cheeks were flushed crimson. His fine suit now seemed as ridiculous to him as a clown's costume.

"I hope I'm not being too much of bother," he stammered. "I didn't mean for Jaina and Jacen to invite me—"

"Don't worry about it," Leia said quickly and smiled. "The ambassador from Karnak Alpha has brought her own brood of children. So please relax. Just do the best you can."

Threepio returned with a kit of grooming implements. "First, we'll comb your hair, young Master Zekk. Everything must be presentable. This is a matter of diplomatic pride for the New Republic, though I do wish I could have located those old files about the customs on Karnak Alpha. The place seems to have been forgotten by my protocol programmers." He fussed over Zekk's hair. "Dear me, you could certainly use a trim! Hmmmm, I wonder if we have time . . ."

Jaina and Jacen came out to greet their friend as he stood soundlessly enduring the golden droid's overattentive ministrations. Jacen's hair seemed awkwardly straight, his face scrubbed so clean that Zekk barely recognized the boy. "Hello, Zekk!" Jaina cried with sincere delight, but when she noticed his outfit she covered her mouth to stifle a giggle. He felt his cheeks burning with fresh shame.

When Zekk struggled against the buzzing device, Threepio said sternly, "I *am* a protocol droid, you know, fully trained in grooming techniques." Zekk didn't argue, but winced as Threepio cleared a snag in his dark hair.

"I'm not sure this is such a good idea," Zekk said. "I don't know anything about diplomacy. I don't know any manners or etiquette."

Jaina laughed. "That's not important. Just use your common sense and watch what the rest of us do. It's a big diplomatic banquet, and you have to follow all sorts of boring ceremonies— but the food's good. You'll enjoy it."

Zekk didn't point out that it was easy for Jaina to say such things, since she had been brought up in this high political society and trained in the proper responses for so many years that such actions were second nature to her. Zekk, though, had no such instruction. This whole dinner was going to be a disaster, he just knew it.

See-Threepio finally gave up on his attempts to comb out Zekk's hair and shook his gleaming head in exasperation. "Oh, dear. I have a bad feeling about this," he sighed. Zekk couldn't argue with him.

Tenel Ka followed the group as they filed toward the formal dining chamber, conscious of her every movement. This was an important diplomatic function, and she had been well tutored by her harsh grandmother in the plush courts of the Hapes Cluster. Tenel Ka was a royal princess, after all, the heir apparent to an entire cluster; but she avoided such nonsense and spent as much as time as possible training instead on her mother's austere world of Dathomir. Tenel Ka's Hapan grandmother strongly disapproved of the path that the princess had chosen to follow, but Tenel Ka had a mind of her own—as she frequently demonstrated.

Now she strode behind Jacen, Jaina, and Zekk, walking next to Lowbacca and the silent younger boy Anakin, as they hurried to the dining chamber. She wore a short, tight-fitting sheath of colorful reptilian hides, freshly oiled and polished so that they gleamed with her every movement. Her muscular arms and legs were bare, but she wore a flowing cape of deep forest green over her shoulders.

Tenel Ka had spent many months at the Jedi academy in the primitive jungles of Yavin 4, and before that she had lived in the cliff cities of the Singing Mountain Clan. It had been a long time since she'd been spoiled with luxuries, but she viewed the formal evening meal with the Karnak ambassador as another challenge to face.

Lowbacca had been shampooed and dried, his fur neatly combed so that he seemed much thinner than usual without his swirling hair sticking out in all directions. The black streak that swept back above his eyebrow had been slicked down, giving him a dashing appearance . . . for a Wookiee.

See-Threepio strutted ahead of Leia and Han as if he were an escort. New Republic guards stood beside the entrance to the great dining hall and swung the doors wide as they approached. Clasping Han Solo's arm, Leia walked in, regal in her fine white robes. Though small of stature, the Chief of State seemed full of energy and confidence, like a battery overcharged with power. Tenel Ka admired her.

Their timing was exactly right. As they passed into the dining hall from one end, the opposite entrance opened, and the ambassador from Karnak Alpha entered, followed by her train of eight children.

The ambassador was a haystack of tan hair, a mound of fur that grew so long that it obscured every other feature of her body. Not even the ambassador's eyes were visible peeping out from between the strands, as she scuttled forward on feet also hidden by her flowing tresses. The ambassador took her place at the head of the table beside the seat reserved for the Chief of State. Leia sat down, with her husband next to her.

The ambassador's children, all eight of them, were miniature versions of her, heaps of hair that bustled to their seats. The girls' fur was knotted into colorful ribbons, while the boys jingled with bells tied to strands of hair. All of them seemed well-groomed and impeccably behaved as they took their seats along one side of the table.

Tenel Ka was glad she had thought to braid colorful ribbons into her own red-gold hair. She had seen natives of Karnak Alpha during her time at the royal court of Hapes. The hairy creatures were shy and had some unusual customs, but they were relatively easygoing.

Tenel Ka sat beside Lowbacca, while Jacen and Jaina took their dark-haired friend Zekk to the front end of the long polished table. Their little brother Anakin, with his eerie ice-blue eyes, seemed content to sit anywhere they directed him, quietly waiting for his place between Lowbacca and Jacen.

See-Threepio moved up and down the line, fussing over items and reveling in his position. This type of duty was, after all, what a protocol droid was programmed for—not for bravery or adventure, but for intricate diplomatic functions.

In front of each gleaming plate sat a crystalline vase containing a cluster of fresh, rich-smelling greens, exotic plants taken from some of Coruscant's botanical gardens—interesting specimens that formed a lovely bouquet for each honored visitor.

Before the start of the meal, Leia gave a carefully rehearsed speech, welcoming the ambassador and expressing her wish for a long and fruitful relationship based on commerce, mutual respect, and support. She whispered to Threepio, and the droid disappeared into an alcove, only to reemerge a moment later carrying a small package. Tenel Ka immediately recognized an incubator sheath wrapped around a smooth ovoid object.

"Hey, that's the hawk-bat egg we rescued!" Jacen said, unable to stop himself.

Leia smiled and nodded. "Yes, and I suppose the ambassador may appreciate the gift even more, now that she knows it was found by the very children she is dining with."

The Karnak ambassador trembled with excitement, her long hair jiggling, as Leia explained. "Madam Ambassador, we know very little about your culture—but we do know that you have a great love for unusual zoological specimens. We have heard reports of your magnificent holographic dioramas and huge alternate-environment zoos where the animals don't even realize they are in a cage. As a diplomatic gift to you and your people, we present to you this rare and precious hawk-bat egg, one of the most difficult-to-catch creatures native to Imperial City. Very few of them are in captivity."

Delighted, the Karnak Alpha ambassador

cooed. "This will surely be a wonderful addition to our rarities."

"But you have to take special care of it," Jacen chided. "I promised its mother personally!"

The hairy ambassador didn't seem to find the comment at all strange. "I give you my solemn promise." Then the ambassador responded with her own rehearsed speech, her mouth moving somewhere between the strands of fur as she echoed the sentiments Leia had expressed.

Meanwhile, her children, little wriggling piles of hair, sat impatient and hungry for the meal, while Jacen, Jaina, and the other young Jedi Knights similarly felt their stomachs growling. Han Solo squirmed restlessly beside Leia in his formal clothes, as if chafing under his stiff collar and his medals of military service. Tenel Ka felt sympathy for him.

See-Threepio came into the room, strutting beside a trundle droid that carried a beaten silver tray of ornate plates piled high with scrumptious-looking cuisine, beautifully garnished and displayed. Out of normal political courtesy, the golden droid marched toward the head of the table while Leia and the Karnak ambassador made the appropriate appreciative sounds, showing how impressed they were with the exquisite food.

Tenel Ka watched See-Threepio move directly toward the ambassador, picking up one of the larger plates from the trundle droid's tray. She knew instantly that Threepio meant to offer the first meal to the ambassador—which was a terribly rude thing to do, according to Karnak custom.

In one quick, fluid motion she sprang to her feet and called across the table. "Excuse me, See-Threepio," she said. "If you would allow me?" She hurried to one end of the table as the droid stopped, completely at a loss as to what to do. One by one, Tenel Ka removed the plates from the tray and reverently set them in front of each of the ambassador's children, starting with the smallest—and presumably the youngest—furball.

Princess Leia looked at Tenel Ka, surprised but reserving judgment. The Karnak ambassador made a motion that must have been a bow of her head. "Why, thank you, young lady. You do us a great honor. This is an unexpected observance of our customs."

Tenel Ka nudged See-Threepio and moved him around to the other side of the table, where she tapped Anakin on the shoulder. She handed the boy a plate, then whispered into his ear. Anakin—without argument or question—stood up, dutifully moved down the table, and presented the next plate of food to the Karnak ambassador.

The ambassador chirped with surprise. "I am most honored, Chief of State," she said to Leia, "that you would choose your youngest to serve me."

"I—thank you," Leia said, uncertain of what else to say.

Tenel Ka stood behind Leia, nodding. Her braided red-gold hair fell forward. "Yes, Ambassador," she said. "We wished to show you honor by respecting the customs of Karnak Alpha— that a young member of the household provides for the guest's children, before a child of the host family serves the most honored adult guest."

"I am most pleased," the ambassador said. "We shall have a simple time making diplomatic treaties, if all members of the New Republic are so considerate of our customs."

Trembling with relief that she had averted what could have been a social gaffe for the Chief of State, Tenel Ka sat back down, while Jacen bent toward her, his brandy-brown eyes wide with astonishment. "How did you know that?" he said in a low whisper.

Tenel Ka shrugged beneath her reptilian armor. "It is . . . just something I learned," she said, and then fell silent, reluctant to reveal her royal upbringing, even to a good friend.

• • •

Even though Zekk sat back and remained quiet, he still felt uncomfortable. The meal tasted delicious, but each time he moved he was afraid that one of his gestures might offend someone or cause a diplomatic incident.

Threepio served the rest of the meals, and Zekk fell to eating with quiet attention, savoring the delicious food . . . though it was far richer than what he was accustomed to.

The salad in the crystal bowl in front of him was crunchy and strange—some of the leaves bitter, others stringy—but he had eaten far worse in his days of scavenging the streets. He had roasted rock slugs and eaten sliced duracrete fungus. These greens at least were fresh, and he relished them.

The conversation around the table seemed to be empty polite chitchat, and Zekk, feeling like an irrelevant guest, did his best to participate. He pushed aside the empty crystal bowl. "Delicious salad," he said. "I don't believe I've ever had greens like that." That sounded good, a complimentary but neutral statement—enough to show willingness to take part in the dinner conversation, yet nothing anyone could fault him for.

Suddenly he felt all eyes turned toward him. He looked down to see if he had spilled something down the front of his out-of-style jacket.

Jacen seemed full of disbelief. Tenel Ka made no sign that she had even heard Zekk's comment. Jaina nudged Zekk with her elbow in a teasing way. "That wasn't a *salad*," she whispered. "That's the *bouquet*. You weren't supposed to eat it."

Zekk listened in horror, but kept his face a careful mask.

See-Threepio spoke up from behind them. "Now then, Mistress Jaina, many plants *are* edible, including all of those within the bouquet. I'm certain there's been no harm—"

From the far end of the table Princess Leia cleared her throat. "I'm glad you liked the salad, Zekk," she said in a voice loud enough for everyone to hear, and pulled her crystal dish toward her. She selected a frilly purple-green leaf and stuffed it in her mouth, munching contentedly. Han Solo looked at his wife as if she had gone crazy, then jerked as if he had been kicked under the table. He too began to eat his bouquet. Jaina followed suit, and soon everyone at the table had devoured their "salads."

Zekk was mortified, though he tried not to show it. His manners were laughable, his clothing was outdated, and he had embarrassed everyone by eating something he should have known was a decoration. He wished he had never been invited to this banquet.

He endured the rest of the evening in simmering silence until the Karnak ambassador and her entourage of furball children finally departed, accompanied by the Chief of State and her husband.

When New Republic escorts came to return them to their rooms, Zekk decided to take the first opportunity to escape.

"Don't worry about tonight, Zekk," Jaina said in an understanding voice. "You're our friend. That's all that matters."

Zekk felt stung by her comment, by the fact that she had even needed to say such a thing. He didn't belong here. That truth was etched in burning letters in his brain. He should have known better, but he had pretended that he could fit in with such high-class friends.

When he slipped out the back door of the main dining hall, fully intending to walk too fast for even the rigid escorts to keep up with him, Jaina tried to stop him. "Wait!" she called. "We're still going to meet tomorrow, right? We promised to help you get that central multitasking unit for Peckhum."

Zekk didn't particularly want to go home, but he certainly couldn't stay. He hurried out into the corridors without answering Jaina.

7

LATER THAT NIGHT, the bulk space cruiser *Adamant* lurched into the Coruscant system, heavily guarded by New Republic warships. The number of assault fighters bristling with turbolaser cannons that clustered around the supply cruiser hinted at the military importance of the cargo it carried.

Standing ready on the cruiser's command bridge, Admiral Ackbar remained tense despite the additional precautions that had been taken. The *Adamant* approached a docking zone near the Coruscant space stations, precisely according to schedule. The assault fighters powered down their weapons and split off as each squadron signaled farewell to the admiral, commander of the New Republic Fleet.

"Thanks for the escort," Ackbar said into the comm unit. "Coruscant security will take over from here." He switched off and paced the bridge. It had been a long haul, but the New Republic badly needed the modern hyperdrive cores and turbolaser battery emplacements his ship carried in its armored holds. The *Adamant* would deliver the components to the Kuat Drive Yards, where they would be installed in a new fleet of battleships. Ackbar had been charged with making a formal inspection tour—and he always relished the chance to be aboard a fine military ship.

Though the main threat from the evil Empire had ended, trouble still flared up in the non-allied systems. The fragile government, led by Chief of State Leia Organa Solo, had to be ready at all times with a force strong enough to ward off attacks from known or unknown enemies.

"Coruscant Central acknowledges our arrival," said the helmsman.

Admiral Ackbar nodded. "It'll be good to take some rest and recreation downside," he said, turning to the helmsman and staring with his round, fishy eyes. "Ever been to Coruscant for a furlough before, Lieutenant?"

The young man nodded. "Yes, sir. Several times. I know where there's this little rooftop cantina, a rotating restaurant that lets you look out across the whole city. They've got a keyboard player with ten tentacles. Boy, you should hear the music she makes!"

Admiral Ackbar chuckled just as the tactical officer turned from her station, her normally pale skin flushed as she shouted an alarm. "Admiral! An unidentified fleet just appeared off our starboard bow. Range is less than fifty kilometers and closing fast. They appear to be in an attack formation."

Ackbar whirled to look out the front viewports. "Attack formation?" he said. "But we're in the Coruscant protected zone, one of the most heavily guarded areas in the galaxy. Who could possibly attack us?" He saw the incoming fleet as it soared in like birds of prey, appearing out of nowhere. In the same moment, he felt the stunning blows from their ion cannons, which immediately crippled the *Adamant*'s defensive systems.

"Battlestations!" he cried in his gravelly voice as another thundering blow slammed into the side of the *Adamant*.

"Minor outer hull breach," the operations officer shouted. "Loss of pressure. Emergency bulkhead doors have closed."

"Transmit a distress signal," Ackbar yelled. "Request immediate assistance from Coruscant security. Now!"

"All weapons systems off-line," the tactical officer reported. "We can't even fire a shot. Engines are still undamaged, though—almost as if our attackers are trying *not* to target them."

"They want to steal this ship," Ackbar said as the cold realization struck him. "And its cargo."

The communications officer had begun transmitting a distress signal, but the round-faced young man looked up almost immediately, his cheeks pale. "Sir, communication systems are nonfunctional. We can't even request help."

Admiral Ackbar swallowed. Coruscant would note the attack and respond within minutes—but by then, he knew, it would be too late.

The enemy ships closed in.

The modified assault shuttle zeroed in on its target. At his controls the former TIE pilot Qorl guided the attack. He wore a black skull-like helmet that sealed against his skin and recirculated breathable air. The dark goggles covering his eyes transmitted important tactical data to his retinas.

He positioned the shuttle's circular cutting "mouth" attachment against the armor plating of the Rebel supply cruiser. The name *Adamant* had been stenciled on the side . . . *Adamant*, which meant impenetrable, unyielding. Qorl grunted to himself. The exceedingly tough cutting teeth were made from industrial-grade Corusca gems and could slice through any known substance. The Shadow Academy's takeover troops would be in control of the ship within moments.

Qorl punched an important-looking red button on the controls. It set the Corusca blades spinning, chewing, until the attachment had sliced out a large circle in the *Adamant*'s hull, opening a hole into the supply cruiser.

Qorl clenched the black-gloved hand of his bulky droid arm into a fist. His own arm had been crippled when his TIE fighter crashed on the jungle moon of Yavin 4, but Imperial engineers had replaced the twisted limb with a more powerful droid attachment. His strength had increased, though he could not feel anything with his new mechanical fingers.

Eager stormtroopers assembled in the boarding tube, holding their blaster rifles ready. Qorl knew that the supply cruiser's main defenses had been on the escort ships, the fourteen heavily armed corvettes, E-wings, and X-wings that had flanked the *Adamant* on its trip to Coruscant. The Rebels had become complacent at their capital world, though, and they had let their defenses lapse for just a moment. Qorl, lurking in his invisible hiding place, had seized that moment to strike.

"Airtight seal complete," a stormtrooper captain reported.

"Very well," Qorl said, standing from his command chair. "Begin the assault. We must be away from here within five standard minutes. We have no time for errors."

The sealed hatch of the boarding tube popped open, and the stormtroopers charged in, firing at anything that moved using only stun beams. They had no particular desire to avoid killing the *Adamant*'s crew, but deadly blaster bolts might cause irreparable damage to the bridge's control systems.

Some of the Rebel crew had taken shelter behind consoles. They fired at the stormtroopers, releasing wild bursts of energy. One trooper went down, a smoking hole in his white chest armor, making a gurgling sound that ended with a burst of static over his comm system.

Qorl marched in, holding a blaster pistol in his droid hand. The stormtroopers fired repeatedly. The Rebel helmsman went down, flying backwards as bolts of blue energy knocked him aside. A tactical officer screamed a challenge as she leaped from her position, shooting four times in quick succession. She killed two stormtroopers before she, too, was stunned.

Qorl strode forward, intent on the *Adamant*'s helm. He needed to get this ship moving soon. The dark goggles of his TIE helmet allowed little peripheral vision, and as he passed the command station, the Rebel commanding officer—a fish-faced Calamarian—leaped up and tackled him. Qorl's blaster pistol clattered to the floor.

The officer wrestled with Qorl, fighting with flipper hands, but the TIE pilot drove his powerful droid fist into the face of the alien, knocking him out cold. Qorl retrieved his blaster pistol and climbed to his feet, brushing off his black uniform.

A stormtrooper captain marched up to him smartly. "The bridge is secure, sir. Ready to move out."

Qorl sat down in the *Adamant*'s command chair. "Very well." He sealed his helmet and his padded suit for total containment, which would protect him from the rapid decompression when the assault ship detached itself from the hull. He hesitated. "Stuff these Rebels into an escape pod, and launch it."

"Save them, sir?" the trooper asked, perplexed. "We don't have much time."

"Then be quick about it!" Qorl snapped. Conflicting emotions warred within him. These were the enemy, and he had sworn to fight them—but the crew on this ship had battled valiantly, and he couldn't stomach letting them die as they lay there unconscious.

The stormtroopers paused for only a second, then hustled as they dragged the limp forms to the bridge escape pod and unceremoniously dumped them inside the defenseless craft. The stormtrooper captain sealed the hatch and punched the pod's external launch control. With a hiss from explosive bolts and a gush of compressed gases, the escape pod shot away.

Qorl studied the *Adamant*'s tactical station. Rebel defensive forces were finally on their way, streaking up out of orbit and heading toward the besieged supply ship. "Go!" he said to the troopers. "Take the assault shuttle and escape. I will meet you back at the base."

The stormtroopers hurried to the shark-mouthed assault shuttle and sealed the boarding hatch. Qorl braced himself as the modified ship detached itself, letting the contained atmosphere rush out of the bridge through the gaping hole, to space.

Secure in his suit, Qorl powered up all the engines. He fed in preprogrammed coordinates, and the *Adamant* lurched into motion. As the Rebel fleet zoomed in, Qorl followed his Imperial ships, carrying with him an incredible treasure that would help the Second Imperium gain its rightful place of military superiority.

The base was very close indeed.

Admiral Ackbar returned to consciousness, and found himself crammed with his crew inside an escape pod that whirled out of control through space. His head ached, and he felt as if a space mine had exploded inside his skull. His crew members groaned and stirred, coming awake. For some reason their lives had been spared. He wriggled his way over to one of the tiny viewports so he could watch for rescue craft.

As the escape pod spun about in a nauseating spiral, Admiral Ackbar saw his own ship from the outside. The hijacked space cruiser *Adamant* lumbered into motion and picked up speed as the Imperial fighters streaked ahead of it.

New Republic reinforcements headed on a direct path to recapture the precious weapons and supplies—but already Ackbar could see that the Imperial ships would be long gone by the time those reinforcements arrived.

Ackbar watched the *Adamant* vanish before the Coruscant ships came close enough to fire a shot. He wished he could just fall back into unconsciousness, but the splitting pain in his skull kept him wide awake.

8

AS ZEKK HURRIED through the night streets of Imperial City, heading away from the palace, he took back stairways and crossed alley catwalks, wanting to see no one. Overhead, blinking lights from shuttles taxiing across the atmosphere fought through a blurring mist of condensed moisture from roof exhaust vents. The city's myriad lights and its sprawling landscape of skyscrapers extending beyond the horizon taunted him with the knowledge that, despite the millions upon millions of inhabitants, he was totally alone.

After the evening's miserable escapades, he felt as if a marquee droid was hovering over his head, broadcasting to everyone that Zekk was a clumsy fool, an embarrassment to his friends. What had he been thinking—trying to fit in with important society, mingling with ambassadors and diplomats, making friends with the children of the Chief of State? Who was *he* to spend time with such people?

He looked at his feet for something to kick, finally spotted an empty beverage container, and lashed out with his boot, a boot he had spent time polishing so he would look good in front of his so-called friends. The container clattered and bounced against a duracrete wall, but to Zekk's frustration it refused to break.

He kept his gaze turned downward, to the shadows and the clusters of garbage in the gutter. He shuffled aimlessly, wandering the back streets, not caring where he might end up. The lower world of Coruscant was his home. He knew it well, and he could survive here—which was good, because it looked as if he would be stuck in this gloomy place for the rest of his life. There was no hope, no chance for advancement. He simply wasn't the equal of those people who could look forward to a bright future—people like Jaina and Jacen.

Zekk was a nobody.

He saw a group of merchants closing up their kiosks for the night, chatting cordially with the New Republic guards who patrolled the streets. Zekk didn't want to go near them, didn't want any company whatsoever. He slipped into a public turbolift and punched a button at random, descending nineteen floors and emerging in a dimmer section of the city.

Old Peckhum had already gone up to the mirror station on his tour of duty, so even Zekk's home would be empty and uninviting. He'd have to spend the night alone, trying to keep amused with games or entertainment systems . . . but nothing sounded at all interesting.

He could wander around for as long as he liked, so he decided to enjoy it. No one would tell him to go to bed, no one would admonish him for going places where he wasn't allowed, no one would breathe down his neck.

He smiled thinly. *He* had a freedom Jaina and Jacen didn't have. When they were out exploring and having fun, the twins constantly checked their chronometers, making sure they would be back home at the appointed time, never making allowances for unexpected circumstances. They certainly didn't want to give their protocol droid a burned worry circuit by not following their explicit orders. The twins were prisoners to their own schedules.

What did it matter if Zekk didn't know all the manners a life in the diplomatic court required? *Who cared* if he didn't understand which eating implement to use, or what the appropriate phrase of gratitude was when speaking to an insectoid ambassador? He snorted with derision. He wouldn't want to live like Jaina and Jacen. No way!

As he wandered along the abandoned corridors, purposely scuffing his toes against the floor plates, he paid no attention to the thickening shadows, to the oppressive silence that surrounded him. He sniffed and clenched his teeth in remembered humiliation. He didn't care about any of that. Zekk was his own person, independent—just the way he liked it.

Overhead, the glowpanels flickered intermittently; those at the far end of the corridor had completely burned out. A skittering sound in the ceiling ducts signaled the passage of a large and clumsy rodent. Ahead he heard another rustling sound, something even bigger.

Zekk looked up with a gasp to see a tall figure, darker than the inky shadows, step out in front of him. "Well, what have we here?" a syrupy voice said, deep and powerful.

The figure stepped closer, and Zekk could see a tall woman with eyes that flashed a burning violet. She wore a glittering black cloak with shoulder spines like defensive armor. Long black hair flowed around her like wire-thin snakes. Her skin was pale, her lips a deep crimson. She tried to smile, but the expression looked foreign on her face.

"Greetings, young sir," she said, her voice oozing persuasion. "I require a moment of your time." When she stepped more fully into the light, Zekk noticed that the woman walked with a pronounced limp.

"I don't think so . . . ," he said, backing up and turning around just as two sinister figures emerged from the side corridors: a compact woman with light brown skin and wavy bronze hair and a shadow-faced young man with dark bushy eyebrows.

"Just one moment of your time, boy. Vilas and Garowyn here will make sure you don't do anything foolish," the dangerous-looking woman said. She limped closer to him. "I am Tamith Kai, and we need to perform a test on you. It won't hurt a bit." Zekk thought he detected a tone of disappointment in her voice.

The young man Vilas and the short, bronze-haired woman grabbed him from behind. Instantly, Zekk struggled, thrashing and shouting out loud. The strangers didn't seem bothered by how much noise he made, and Zekk knew with a sinking certainty that cries for help were not at all uncommon in these abandoned levels—although brave rescuers were.

Zekk tried to yank his arms free from the clawlike grasp of his captors, but to no avail. Tamith Kai withdrew a strange device from the black folds of her cape. Unraveling wires connected to a pair of flat crystalline paddles, she switched on an additional power grid. A high-pitched hum vibrated through the machine case.

"Leave me alone!" Zekk lashed backward with his foot, hoping to deliver a sharp blow to sensitive shins.

"Be careful," Tamith Kai said to her colleagues with a meaningful scowl. "Some of them can be dangerous when they kick."

She leaned closer and waved the humming crystal paddles around his body, scanning him. His heart pounding with fear, Zekk gritted his teeth and squeezed his emerald eyes shut. To his surprise, he felt no tingling energy; no burning analytical beam sliced through his skin.

Tamith Kai withdrew, and Garowyn and Vilas leaned over Zekk's bony shoulders to observe the readings. Still struggling, Zekk caught a glimpse of the glowing image, a colorful aura projected in a micro-hologram.

"Hmmm, surprising," Tamith Kai said. "Look at the power he has."

"A good find," Garowyn agreed. "Quite fortunate."

"Not fortunate for me!" Zekk snapped. "What do you want?"

"You'll be coming with us," Tamith Kai said. Her tone was filled with confidence, as if she didn't care about his objections.

"I'm not going *anywhere* with you!" Zekk shouted. "No matter what you found, I won't—"

"Oh, just stun him," Tamith Kai said impatiently, turning about on her stiff leg and limping back down the shadow-shrouded corridor. "He'll be easier to carry that way."

Vilas released his grip on the boy's arms, and Zekk tried to run, knowing this was his last chance . . . but arcs of blue fire looped out, engulfing him and slamming him down into unconsciousness.

9

JAINA STARED MOROSELY at her brothers. She bit her lip, wondering what their mother would say when she got back from seeing the Karnak Alpha ambassador to her quarters. She hoped Leia wasn't too upset with Zekk.

Jacen paced the living area, muttering to himself. "Blaster bolts!" he said with a dramatic gesture. "Can you believe Zekk thinking the bouquet was a salad? It's a good thing Tenel Ka was there to head off that other problem. We still probably made a terrible impression on the ambassador."

"I don't think it turned out so badly," Anakin said from where he sat on a large cushion near the door. "Mom will handle it. You'll see."

Jaina groaned. "Zekk probably feels terrible."

"We'll see him in the morning," Jacen said, "when we help him look for that central multi-tasking unit. We can apologize to him then."

The door to their quarters swished open and Leia walked in wearing a bemused expression. After a moment of anxious silence, all three of her children spoke at once.

"I'm sorry, Mom. It's all my fault," Jaina blurted.

"Was the ambassador very angry?" Jacen asked.

"Where's Dad?" Anakin said.

The barrage of questions snapped Leia out of her daze. "Nothing to be sorry for, Jaina," she said, giving her daughter a hug. "The ambassador says I've got three wonderful children, and they have charming friends." She stooped to smooth back Anakin's straight dark hair. "And to answer *your* question, your father had begun discussing hyperspace trade routes to Karnak Alpha with the ambassador, and decided to stay for some business that was even more important."

Jaina blinked in surprise at this unexpected turn of events and sat down at one end of a long, cushioned repulsorseat. Leia sat down beside her, and Jacen settled next to his mother on the other end of the seat. Leia adjusted the repulsorseat's controls to a gentle rocking motion. Anakin dragged his floor cushion over to sit beside them, quiet and attentive.

Leia smiled down at her children. "The ambassador was certainly impressed by the number of young people we had invited to meet her at the dinner. She also said that any adult who was willing to break with her own social traditions just to make a child feel more comfortable should have no problem negotiating an alliance with Karnak Alpha. I'm glad you twins were here with us, rather than at the Jedi academy."

"That's great, Mom," said Jaina, snuggling deeper into the cushions.

"I learned something very important about myself tonight," Leia continued. "As your father and I walked the ambassador and her children back to their quarters, I realized that *my* kids were more important to me than any ambassador. When we got to their quarters, the ambassador said she was ready to discuss her planet's alliance with the New Republic. That's when I amazed even myself. I said I'd be happy to talk with her about it in the morning—but that for right now I needed to be with my children."

Jaina gave a low whistle. Her mother was always so wrapped up in her duties as Chief of State, such a response seemed inconceivable. "You didn't!"

Leia chuckled. "Yes I did, and you know what she said?" She sounded a bit surprised. "She said in that case she no longer had any doubts that we could form an alliance. Everything is all set."

"If everything's all set, why didn't Dad come back with you?" Anakin asked. "What other important business was there?"

"He offered to stay behind," Leia said, raising her eyebrows, "and tell the ambassador's children one of your favorite bedtime stories. Can you guess which one?"

Jacen, Jaina, and Anakin all murmured in unison, "The Little Lost Bantha Cub."

"Then you'll have to tell us a story, too, Mom," Anakin said in a sleepy voice.

So she did.

10

THE NEXT MORNING, as they found their way through the streets, Jacen had an uneasy prickly feeling at the back of his neck, as if a trail of mermyns were crawling along his skin. Something felt wrong, but he couldn't quite put his finger on what it was. "Blaster bolts," he muttered.

For some reason they all seemed a bit jumpy today. Jaina had taken the lead, since she was most familiar with the way to Zekk's quarters. Jacen, on the other hand, always got lost. Tenel Ka followed Jaina in silence, her shoulders squared, her back rigid, while Jacen and Lowie brought up the rear.

They trooped through the ancient cramped alleyways of metal and stone. The lights were too dim in this area, and the air tasted of rusting metal and decay. Even the odors were unfamiliar and, to Wookiees at least—judging by the wrinkling of Lowie's nose—none too pleasant.

"Here we are," Jaina said, rounding a sharp corner into an even narrower passageway. She stopped at a low doorway and pressed the signal button. The indicator light flashed red, denying them access. Jaina bit her lower lip. "That's strange. Zekk said yesterday that he'd clear us for access."

"Perhaps he is more upset than we expected," Tenel Ka suggested.

"Maybe," Jaina agreed, "but not likely. Zekk doesn't break promises. We've had disagreements before, but . . ." Her voice trailed off.

When Lowbacca rumbled a comment, Em Teedee translated. "Master Lowbacca wonders if Master Zekk might not simply have stepped out for a morning constitutional. Or perhaps he decided to procure comestibles for morning meal."

"Yeah, that would be better than those stormtrooper rations he gave us last time," Jacen pointed out, feeling his stomach gurgle with distaste at the thought.

"He knew we were coming," Jaina said. "He should have been here."

"Let's wait for a while," Jacen suggested, sitting with crossed legs on the floor. "He'll probably turn up in a few minutes with some wild story."

"That would be just like him," Jaina agreed.

Jacen, knowing his sister was still worried, tried to sound as confident as possible. "He'll be back any minute—you'll see. In the meantime," he suggested brightly, "I've got some new jokes, if anybody wants to hear them."

The twins entertained the other young Jedi Knights with stories of Zekk's past adventures. Jacen told about the time Zekk climbed forty-two stories down an abandoned turbolift shaft because he saw something glittery and reflective by the glow of his pulsed-laser spotlight. Imagining treasures that grew more and more extravagant with each level he descended, Zekk discovered in the end that the shining object was merely a discarded foil wrapping stuck to the ooze dripping along the shaft wall.

Jaina shared a story about how Zekk reprogrammed a personal translating device for a group of snide reptilian tourists who had shoved him out of line for free samples of a new food product. Zekk changed their translator so that every time the reptilian tourists asked for directions to eating establishments or museums, they were instead guided to seedy gambling parlors or garbage-reprocessing stations.

"How simply dreadful!" Em Teedee commented.

Minutes crept by and became an hour, and still their friend did not return.

At last Jaina stood. "Something's wrong," she said, biting her lower lip. "Zekk's not coming."

Lowie growled and Em Teedee translated, "Master Lowbacca suggests that perhaps Master Zekk requires a certain amount of time to overcome his embarrassment. I don't suppose I'll ever understand human behavior," he added.

"Maybe," Jaina said, her face troubled and unconvinced.

"Hey, why don't we leave a videonote," Jacen suggested. "We'll try again tomorrow. How long can he stay mad at us?"

But the next day Zekk was still nowhere to be found. Jacen pressed the access request button beside Zekk's front door, but again there was no response. Old Peckhum would be returning from the mirror station soon, and he would come home to an empty apartment.

"I think it's time to start looking for Zekk," Jacen said, staring at the blank infopanel.

"Agreed," Tenel Ka said.

"Well then," Jaina said, rubbing her hands together briskly, "what are we waiting for? And if we still can't find him, we'll talk to Mom."

• • • •

Leia Organa Solo seemed preoccupied and concerned as they entered her private office. Leia smiled at them and brushed a stray hair out of Jaina's eyes. "I'm glad you're here, kids. I wanted to show you something."

Before Jacen or Jaina could tell her about Zekk, Leia played a grainy long-range videoclip that showed Imperial attack vessels striking a New Republic military supply cruiser in space near Coruscant.

"That looks like the ship that kidnapped us from Lando's GemDiver Station!" Jaina cried.

Lowbacca growled in agreement.

Leia nodded. "I thought so, from your description—and now I can confirm it to Admiral Ackbar. This attack came two nights ago. We may have a real threat on our hands, right here on the capital world."

Jaina watched the videoclip again and frowned. "Something else isn't right about those images. I'm trying to figure out what. . . ."

Leia returned to her desk. "Admiral Ackbar and a handful of tactical experts are analyzing the footage, and they might want to ask you some questions. We're stepping up security against the very real possibility that we may see another Imperial attack."

After that news, when Jacen poured out the story of Zekk's disappearance, Leia didn't seem overly concerned. She let her gaze drift across all four of the young Jedi Knights standing in her office. "All right, let me ask you this: Who knows the city better, the four of you . . . or Zekk?"

"Well, Zekk does," Jacen answered in a hesitant voice. "But—"

"And if Zekk is upset and hiding somewhere," Leia continued, "is it any wonder that you haven't been able to find him?"

"But he wouldn't do that," Jaina objected. "He promised us."

"Well then," Leia said in a calm, reasonable voice, "maybe he's found that central multitasking unit already and Peckhum shuttled him up to the mirror station."

"But he would have left us a message." Jaina set her mouth in a stubborn line.

"She's right, Mom," Jacen spoke up. "Zekk may seem like a scamp, but he always does what he says he's going to do."

Leia swept her children with a skeptical look. "How many years have we known Zekk?"

Jaina shrugged. "About five, but what—"

"And in those years," Leia went on, "how many times has he just disappeared on some adventure, only to reappear about a month later?"

Jacen cleared his throat and shifted uncomfortably. "Um, maybe half a dozen times."

"There. You see?" Leia said, as if that closed the matter.

"But those other times," Jacen pointed out, "we didn't have plans to spend the day with him."

Leia sighed. "And those other times he wasn't upset over an embarrassing diplomatic dinner, either. Look, he's older than you are, and legally he can come and go as he pleases. But even if we knew for certain that he was missing—which we don't—there's very little we could do about it. The galaxy is a big place. Who knows where he might be?

"People turn up missing all the time, and we simply don't have the resources to look for everybody. Just this week I've had reports of at least three other teenagers missing in Imperial City alone. Why don't you wait and talk to Peckhum when he gets back tomorrow? Maybe he'll have some ideas." She herded them out of the room so she could get back to work.

"Right now I've got to get ready for my next meeting with the Karnak Alphan ambassador. And then I have to see the Howler Tree People again for a musical ceremony this afternoon. . . ." She rubbed her temples as if in anticipation of a headache. "I really do love my job—uh, most of it at least."

As they left Leia's office, Jacen groaned. "Mom doesn't believe there's even a problem."

"Then I guess we'll have to keep searching on our own," Jaina said.

Lowie growled agreement.

"It's all up to us," Jacen said, pounding a determined fist into his palm.

"This is a fact," said Tenel Ka.

11

AFTER WHAT SEEMED like an eternity, Zekk fought his way back to consciousness. He felt as if a million volts had shot through his body, short-circuiting half of his nerves and leaving his muscles tingly and twitching.

His head ached. The hard metal floor beneath his body oozed a cruel chill. The harsh white light hurt his eyes.

When he sat up, he had to blink away sparkling, colored spots. Waiting for his vision to focus, Zekk finally realized there was nothing to *see*—only blank, whitish-gray walls. He found a small speaker grille and the vent for an air-circulation system, but nothing else. He couldn't even find the door.

Zekk knew he must be in some kind of cell. He remembered struggling with the evil-looking people who had captured him in the lower city—a black-haired woman with violet eyes using a strange scanning device, and a dark young man who had stunned him. . . .

"Hey!" he yelled. His voice sounded rough and hoarse. "Hey! Where am I?" He got to his feet, swaying from dizziness, and made his way to the nearest wall. He hammered on the metal plates, shouting for attention. He worked his way around the small room, but found no door crack.

He stumbled to the speaker and shouted into it. "Somebody tell me what's going on. You have no right to take me prisoner!"

But in spite of his brave words, Zekk knew things that Jaina and Jacen, raised within the protective confines of the law and guarded by security forces all their lives, had never understood. Zekk knew that his "rights" wouldn't be protected if someone had the power to take them away. No one would fight for *him*. No one would send military fleets to rescue *him*. If Zekk disappeared, there would be no public outcry. Few people would even notice.

"Hey!" he shouted again, kicking at the wall. "Why am I a prisoner? Why do you want *me*?"

He whirled as he heard a whishing sound on the opposite side of the room. A smooth door slid aside to reveal a powerful-looking man flanked by stormtroopers. The man was tall and wore silvery robes. His hair was blond and neat, his face gentle and complacent. His exceedingly handsome features looked as finely made as a sculpture. The man's very presence exuded an aura of peace and calm.

"Aren't you overreacting a bit?" the man said. His rich voice hummed with power and charisma. "We came as soon as we realized you were awake. You could have hurt yourself by pounding so hard on the walls."

Zekk did not allow himself to relax. "I want to know why I'm here," he said. "Let me go. My friends will be looking for me."

"No they won't." The man shook his head. "We have enough information about you to know that. But don't worry."

"Don't worry?" Zekk sputtered. "How can you say—" He stopped short, as the man's words struck home. No, his friends wouldn't be looking for him, would they? He doubted Jaina and Jacen would want to be seen with him after the debacle of the diplomatic banquet. "What do you mean?" he asked in a subdued voice.

The man in the silvery robes gestured to the guards. The stormtroopers waited outside as the man entered the cell alone, sealing the door behind him. "I see they put you in our . . . least extravagant living quarters." He sighed. "We'll find you a more comfortable room as soon as possible."

"Who are you?" Zekk said, still not letting his guard down. "Why did you stun me?"

"My name is Brakiss, and I apologize for the . . . enthusiasm of my colleague Tamith Kai. But I do believe she authorized the use of force only because of your struggles. If you had cooperated, it could have been a much more pleasant experience."

"I didn't know being kidnapped was supposed to be 'pleasant,'" Zekk snarled.

"Kidnapped?" Brakiss said in feigned alarm. "Let's not jump to conclusions until we've got the full story."

"Then explain it to me," Zekk said.

"All right." Brakiss smiled. "Would you like any refreshments? Something warm to drink?"

"Just tell me what's going on," Zekk said.

Brakiss pressed his hands together. His silvery robes flickered around him like rippling water under a cloudy sky. "I have some news for you—good news, I hope you'll agree, although it may come as something of a shock."

"What?" Zekk asked, frowning skeptically.

"Are you aware that you have Jedi potential?"

Zekk's green eyes widened. "Jedi—me? I think you've got the wrong person."

Brakiss grinned. "Fairly *strong* potential. We were surprised ourselves. Didn't your friends Jacen and Jaina tell you? Weren't you aware?"

"I don't have any Jedi potential," Zekk mumbled. "I couldn't have anything like that."

"And why not?" Brakiss asked, raising his eyebrows. He seemed so reasonable. He waited for Zekk to answer, and finally the boy looked down at his hands.

"Because I . . . I'm just a street kid. I'm a nobody. Jedi Knights are great protectors of the New Republic. They're powerful and . . ."

Brakiss nodded impatiently. "Yes they are—but the *potential* to be a Jedi has nothing to do with where you live or how you were raised. The Force knows no economic boundaries. Luke Skywalker himself was just the foster son of a moisture farmer.

"Why shouldn't a poor kid like you have just as much Jedi ability as, for instance, a politician's twin children who live in luxury with all their needs cared for? In fact," Brakiss said in a lower voice, "it could be that because your life has been so tough, your true potential as a Jedi has been honed even sharper than the potential of those pampered little brats."

"They're not brats," Zekk retorted. "They're my friends."

Brakiss dismissed his comment with a casual wave. "Whatever."

"How come I never knew about this? How come I never . . . felt anything?" Zekk asked.

He realized suddenly what Tamith Kai had been scanning for with her strange electronic device.

Brakiss rocked back on his heels. "You might not know you had any Force talent if no one ever trained you. It's a simple enough thing to measure, though. If Jacen and Jaina were such close friends, I'm shocked to think that they never *bothered* to test you. Isn't it true that Master Skywalker is desperately on the lookout for more Jedi Knights?"

Zekk nodded uncomfortably.

"Well, if that's so," Brakiss continued, "why didn't they test everyone around them? Why would they just dismiss you out of hand, Zekk? I think they've shortchanged you; they probably never even *imagined* that a street kid, a lowborn scamp, would be worthy of Jedi training, no matter what his innate potential."

"That isn't it," Zekk muttered, but his words carried no strength.

"Have it your way." Brakiss shrugged.

Zekk looked away, though the featureless walls of the cell gave him nothing else to stare at. He waved a hand around to indicate the cold, close cell. "What is this place?" he asked, trying to change the subject.

"This place is the Shadow Academy," Brakiss said, and Zekk was startled to recognize the name of the hidden station where Jaina and Jacen had been held against their will. "I am in charge of training new Jedi for the Second Imperium. I use different methods than Master Skywalker follows at his Yavin 4 training center." Brakiss frowned sympathetically. "But then you wouldn't know, would you? Your friends never took you there." His voice turned up in a question. "Did they? Even for a visit?"

Zekk shook his head.

"Well, *I* am training new Jedi, powerful warriors to help bring back the glory and order of a new Empire. The Rebel Alliance is a criminal movement. You wouldn't understand that, because you're too young to remember what it was like under Emperor Palpatine."

"I hate the Empire!" Zekk said.

"No you don't," Brakiss assured him. "Your friends have *told* you to hate the Empire, but you never witnessed any of it firsthand. You've only seen their version of history. You realize, of course, that whichever government is in charge always makes the defeated enemy look like a monster. I will tell you the truth. The Empire had very little political chaos. Every person had opportunities. There were no gangs running wild through the streets of Coruscant. Everyone had a task to do, and they did it willingly.

"Besides, what does galactic politics have to

do with you, young Zekk? You've never been concerned with such things. Would your life really change if the Chief of State were replaced by a different politician in a different Empire? If you work with us, on the other hand, your life could be much improved."

Zekk shook his head, clamping his teeth together. "I won't betray my friends," he growled.

"Your friends," Brakiss said. "Oh, yes . . . the ones who never tested you for Jedi potential, the ones who only come to visit you when it fits into their social schedule. They're going to leave you behind, you know, as they find more 'important' work to do. They'll forget about you so fast you won't have time to blink."

"No," Zekk whispered. "No they won't."

"Tell me, what does the future hold for you?" Brakiss continued, his voice persuasive. "Certainly, you've made friends that move in rich and important circles—but will you ever be a part of that? Be honest with yourself."

Zekk didn't answer, though he knew the truth deep in his heart.

"You'll be scavenging for the rest of your years, selling trinkets to earn enough credits for your next meal. Do you really have any chance for power or glory or importance of your *own*?"

Again, Zekk refused to answer. Brakiss leaned forward, his beautifully chiseled features radiating kindness and concern. "I'm offering you that chance, boy. Are you brave enough to take it?"

Zekk searched for the strength to resist, focused on a thread of anger. "The same chance you offered to Jaina and Jacen? They told me how you kidnapped them, brought them to the Shadow Academy, and tortured them."

"Tortured them?" Brakiss laughed and shook his blond head. "I suppose after being pampered all their lives, a bit of hard work might *seem* like torture. I offered to train them to become powerful Jedi—I admit it was a mistake. We wanted young Jedi Knights to train, but the candidates we invited were too high-profile. The risk was greater than we had anticipated, and it called too much attention to our academy.

"So I decided to change my plan. As I told you, the Force moves as strongly within the less-fortunate as in those who are rich and powerful. Your social status doesn't concern *me* in the least, Zekk—only your talent and your willingness to develop it. Tamith Kai and I have decided to search among the lower levels of society for people whose potential is just as great as in those among the higher levels, and yet whose disappearance won't cause such a stir. People with the incentive to work with us."

Zekk scowled, but Brakiss's eyes blazed. "If you join us, I guarantee you the name of Zekk will never be ignored or forgotten."

The cell door opened again, and a stormtrooper held out a tray with steaming beverages and delicious-looking pastries. "Let's have a snack while we keep talking," Brakiss said. "I trust most of your questions have been answered, but feel free to ask anything else you wish."

Zekk realized that he was voraciously hungry, and he took three of the pastries, licking his lips as he ate them. He had never tasted anything so wonderful in his life.

The implications of Brakiss's words terrified him, but the questions about his future bubbled to the surface again and again in his mind. Although Zekk didn't want to admit it, he could not shake the feeling that Brakiss and his promises made a lot of sense.

As Brakiss sealed the door behind him on his way out, he turned to the stormtrooper guards in the hall. "See that the boy gets a nicer room," he said. "I don't think we'll have much trouble with him."

The master of the Shadow Academy glided

down the corridor as the old TIE pilot marched up to report. Qorl was still in his black armored suit and cradled his skull-like helmet in his powerful droid arm. "The captured Rebel cruiser *Adamant* is now enclosed within our shields, Lord Brakiss," he said. "Its weaponry is being off-loaded even as we speak."

Brakiss smiled broadly. "Excellent. Was it as big a shipment as we expected?"

Qorl nodded. "Affirmative, sir. The hyperdrive cores and turbolaser batteries will enable us to virtually double the Second Imperium's military strength. It was a wise move to strike now."

Brakiss folded his hands together, letting his flowing silvery sleeves swallow them up. "Most excellent. Everything is proceeding as planned. I will report to our Great Leader and tell him the good news. Before long, the Empire will shine again—and these Rebels can do nothing to prevent it."

12

"SHUTTLE *MOON DASH*, this is Coruscant Control Tower One. You are cleared to leave spacedock. Bay doors opening in Gamma Section."

Captain Narek-Ag opened her main comm channel. "Thank you, Tower One. This is shuttle *Moon Dash*, heading for Gamma bay doors with a full load of cargo." She switched off the comm unit and grinned conspiratorially at her copilot, Trebor. "A few more good payloads like this," she said, "and I may just ask you to marry me." Her hazel eyes held a teasing look.

Trebor grinned back, accustomed to his captain's sense of humor. "Keep making good business deals like this one, and I may just accept."

With the ease born of long practice, Narek guided her shuttle out of its docking bay in one of Coruscant's orbiting space stations. "Coordinates locked in?" she asked.

"Locked in and confirmed," her copilot answered the moment she finished speaking.

Narek chuckled as her shuttle streaked away from the spacedock. Accelerating through the inner Coruscant system, she calibrated their hyperspace path for Bespin, the next planet on their run. "You know, for a small-time operation—"

"—we're not half bad," Trebor finished for her.

"Not half bad," she echoed with a satisfied nod. "Calculating hyperspace path."

"Almost ready," Trebor said. "If we hurry, there might be enough time to deliver this cargo to Cloud City and still arrange for a second payload on the return trip. That would double our profit for this run."

A pleased smile spread across Narek's face. She flicked her auburn hair to one side. "I love it when you think like a businessman."

"Business*person*," Trebor corrected. "Approaching top acceleration. Prepare for jump to lightspeed."

Suddenly the *Moon Dash* lurched as if it had slammed into an impenetrable barrier. The tiny craft ricocheted, spinning uncontrollably. Alarms whooped and bright warning lights flashed across the control console.

"What was that?" Narek demanded, shaking her head to clear the blurry spots from her vision. She stared out the viewport at empty space.

"I don't know!" Trebor said. "Nothing showed up on the sensors. Nothing showed up on the sensors! It's supposed to be clear space!"

"Well, it's the *hardest* piece of clear space I've ever encountered," Narek-Ag shot back. "Damage report!"

"Not sure. Can you get us stabilized?" her copilot asked. "Okay, looks like we got a lower hull rupture. Awww, there goes all our cargo! Engines running beyond the red lines." He swallowed. "We are in deep trouble, lady."

Then, as if to emphasize Trebor's assessment, a shower of sparks erupted from the main guidance console. *Moon Dash* careened out of control.

"Emergency, Coruscant One! This is shuttle *Moon Dash*. We've struck unknown space debris," Trebor yelled into the comm unit. A burst of static from the speaker grille was accompanied by a squeal of feedback and another spray of sparks.

Narek-Ag coughed and tried to wave away the smoke. She flicked a pair of switches. "Aft-thrusters not responding," she said in a terse voice. "Still scanning the area—there's *nothing*. What did we smash into?"

"News ain't any better from where I sit," Trebor said. "Can't get much worse."

"It can't, huh? Well, it just did," Narek said with a hard gulp. "I guess I'd better ask you to marry me after all."

Trebor caught sight of the readout that had grabbed his captain's attention. He groaned aloud. An unstoppable chain reaction had begun to build inside their engine chambers like an avalanche of deadly energy. Within seconds, the *Moon Dash* would explode like a small supernova.

"Always wanted to get married out among the stars," he said. Tears stung his eyes. Probably from the acrid smoke, he thought. "Never had a better offer." He placed his hand over hers. "I accept . . . but I have to say that your timing stinks."

She squeezed his hand, then looked down at the panels. "Uh-oh! Hyperdrive engines are going crit—"

In space, the *Moon Dash* erupted in a silent shower of molten metal and flaming gases, fading to black.

Jaina paced the main living area of her family's quarters in the Imperial Palace like a caged jungle creature she had seen once in the Holographic Zoo for Extinct Animals. She hated inactivity. She wanted to *do* something.

Jacen and Tenel Ka had gone out again to look for Zekk, taking along See-Threepio and Anakin, while Lowie was off working with his uncle Chewbacca. When Jacen had pointed out that it would be a good idea for someone to stay behind in case Zekk or Peckhum tried to reach them, Jaina had reluctantly agreed to be the one.

She had finally broken down and tried to contact old Peckhum up in the mirror station, though he was due to return home that day. At his station holo panel, Peckhum had answered right away, but as she started to explain that Zekk had disappeared, the old man's fuzzy image quickly deteriorated. His response was all but drowned out by static. ". . . can't understand your . . . not receivi . . . transmission . . . returning tonight . . ."

The station's central multitasking unit was getting progressively worse, and communication wouldn't be possible until she saw Peckhum face-to-face.

By the time her mother came home for midday meal, Jaina was ready to scream from just sitting around. She was eager to talk, but Leia's face seemed tired and careworn, and Jaina decided it was best not to intrude on her mother's thoughts. She brought Leia a warm lunch from the processing station and sat down to eat beside her in silence.

A few minutes later Han Solo dashed in and rushed over to his wife. "I came as soon as I got your message. What is it?"

A grateful smile lifted the corners of Leia's mouth as she looked at her husband. "I need to get your opinion on something," she said. "Do you have time to sit down and eat with us?"

Han flashed her a roguish grin. "Midday meal with the two most beautiful women in the galaxy? Of course I've got time. What happened? Another disaster like the Imperial attack?" He helped himself to a bowl of warm Corellian stew.

"A disaster all right." Leia took a deep breath. "A shuttle blew up this morning just as it was leaving orbit."

Jaina looked up in surprise, but her father nodded. "Yeah, I heard about it an hour ago."

Leia's brows drew together in a frown of concentration. "No one seems to know what happened. What could have caused something like that?"

"Poor maintenance?" Jaina suggested. "Engine overload?"

Leia looked troubled again. "Coruscant One picked up a transmission just before the *Moon Dash* exploded. The captain seemed to think they'd run into something."

Han's eyebrows shot up. "Still in outer orbit,

you mean? Any other ships around that weren't cleared for takeoff?"

"Noooo . . ." Leia said slowly.

"A space mine deliberately planted there? Or a piece of debris?"

Jaina's ears perked up. "We ran into a lot of debris on our way home this time, didn't we, Dad?"

Leia grimaced. "I was afraid of that. The Commissioner of Trade has taken this personally. He says that all the leftover wreckage in orbit over Coruscant has always been an accident waiting to happen. He insists that we give higher priority to plotting safer space lanes. We've mapped out some of the bigger pieces, but I think quite a few chunks escaped our surveys—and we haven't had time to check it. Some of that wreckage has been up there in orbit for decades."

Han pursed his lips. "These accidents are pretty rare, Leia. Let's not overreact."

"According to the *Moon Dash*'s transmissions, they never saw what hit them—and it wasn't on any map. The Commissioner considers this an important safety issue. I have to agree—in the wake of this accident, we need to do something about it."

"How much work would it be to map the orbits of the larger pieces of wreckage?" Han asked.

"Quite a bit. And time-consuming, too." Leia pinched the bridge of her nose as if she had suddenly been assailed by another headache. "I'm not even sure the New Republic has resources to commit to a project like that—"

"Maybe I could help," Jaina interrupted, fixing her interest on an idea that would take her mind off Zekk. "After all, Uncle Luke said we were supposed to choose a study project while we're away from the academy. Lowie and I could map the debris for you. It sounds like fun."

Jaina looked from the datapad to the computer screen, then at the holographic simulation. "Okay, this is the next trajectory, Lowie." She stretched, trying to loosen the knotted muscles in her shoulders, then rubbed her bleary eyes, but her vision did not clear. They had been at the task for hours. She couldn't imagine why she had ever thought it would be fun.

The lanky Wookiee carefully programmed the orbit she had indicated, and another glowing streak appeared on the holomap. Jaina groaned. "This may be an important job, but I sure thought it would be more interesting."

Lowie grumbled a reply, and Em Teedee translated. "Master Lowbacca maintains that—

although plotting swarms of orbital debris never *should* have seemed an interesting project in the first place—schoolwork is rarely interesting. This job, at least, carries a certain amount of urgency." Lowie growled another comment. "Furthermore, he points out that the project is only approximately twelve percent complete, and he will be most gratified when it is finished."

Jaina sighed wearily and ran her hands through her straight brown hair. "Well then," she said, "what are we waiting for?"

13

PECKHUM SHIFTED THE strap of the travel duffel to his other shoulder as he trudged away from the *Lightning Rod*'s low-rent docking station, where many smugglers and con artists also parked their ships. It was good to be back in the city, if only because the equipment *worked* in his apartment, which was more than he could say about the facilities aboard the mirror station.

Despite his heavy pack, the grizzled old man slid through the broad streets and narrow alleyways with unconscious ease, muttering to himself as he went. "'You'll just have to make do, Peckhum.' 'We've got procurement problems, Peckhum.' 'New equipment is expensive, Peckhum.' 'Central multitasking units don't grow on starflower vines, Peckhum.'" Scratching at his chin stubble with one hand, he continued to rant, as used to talking to himself as he was to talking to Zekk.

He growled. "You'd think they'd at least wait till I got off my ship to tell me the news. 'We tried to reach you, Peckhum, but we couldn't get through.' Serves 'em right, since they haven't fixed my comm system!" He shifted his duffel again. "'Your replacement was reassigned to an additional security detail due to the recent Imperial attack, Peckhum. We need you back at the station tomorrow, Peckhum.' Hah!"

He stomped ahead, hardly noticing the cheery merchants, the wide-eyed tourists, the self-absorbed civil servants. "I just wish the administrator in charge of the mirror station would stop sitting in his comfy office down here and go up for a field trip. Feed him some of the swill the food-prep units have been putting out and see how much *he* likes it! See how well *he'd* 'make do.'"

Peckhum turned a corner and made his way down the corridor toward his home. "If I waited for those bureaucrats to get something done, why, the whole station would fall apart." Then he smiled at the thought of Zekk's promise of a new central multitasking unit. "Sometimes you just gotta do things for yourself . . . with a little help from your friends."

Peckhum looked up with satisfaction to find

himself at his door. He keyed in the unlocking code, and the door slid open with a *whoosh* of escaping air. The air smelled stale and musty, as if it had been recycled over and over again for days. He'd have to remind Zekk to let in some fresh air now and then.

He tossed his duffel inside the front entryway, as the door sealed itself behind him. No friendly voice rang out to greet him. "Hey, Zekk!" he called. The apartment seemed oppressively silent, so he raised his voice a bit. "After three days of breathing from bad tanks on the mirror station, even *this* air smells good, but . . ." He paused. There was no response. "Zekk?"

He looked around the cluttered main living area, then searched the food-prep chamber, Zekk's bedroom, even the refresher unit. All empty.

A concerned frown crinkled Peckhum's forehead. Zekk rarely went out when he knew Peckhum was returning from a job—especially not when he had promised to deliver a piece of scavenged equipment. But Peckhum saw no sign of the central multitasking unit. He would need it before the next morning's trip back up to the station.

He scratched his cheeks again and thought for a moment. Then he relaxed. "Of course," he said to himself, "the Solo kids."

Zekk's friends Jacen and Jaina would be on Coruscant for only a few weeks. They were probably all out somewhere, enjoying themselves, telling tall tales of their adventures on other planets. Glancing back, he noticed the winking light on the infopanel beside the front door. That meant some messages hadn't been picked up yet. Probably just Zekk letting him know where he and his friends were, Peckhum thought.

There were three messages in all. Peckhum reviewed them. The first message showed the image of Jaina and Jacen Solo, standing with the other two young Jedi Knights.

"Hey, Zekk," Jacen said in his characteristically good-humored voice. "We came to go on the scavenger hunt with you for that unit Peckhum needs. It was this morning, wasn't it? We'll come by again tomorrow morning. Let us know if there's a change of plans."

As the next message played, Jaina Solo appeared, her hair straight and her expression concerned. "Zekk, it's us. Are you all right? We've been looking for you everywhere! I'm sorry if you still feel bad about the other night—it's okay, really. Can you call us when you get home?"

The final message showed Jaina again, her face anxious and drawn. She spoke slowly, as if each of her words stuck in her throat. "Zekk, are you upset about anything? We're all really . . . sorry if we said anything to make you feel uncomfortable at the banquet. If you've already found that central multitasking unit and you don't want to take us scavenger hunting with you right now, we'll understand. Please talk to us, if you get this message."

As Peckhum listened, his stomach contracted with dread. Something had to be wrong. He looked around again, seeing no signs that the boy had planned to leave. No messages. No notes.

That was unlike Zekk. He was more reliable than that. Others might brush him off as a young scoundrel or a street urchin, but Zekk knew his responsibilities well and always met them. He had promised Peckhum a new central multitasking unit, knowing how important it was to the mirror station. If Zekk told him he was going to do something, the boy did it. Always.

Sure, Zekk was an orphan, a joker, a teller of tall tales, an adventurer—but he had always been a good friend, and he had always been completely reliable.

Almost before he knew it, his decision was made. Stopping only to leave a brief videomessage for Zekk on the infopanel, just in case the boy came back, he headed out the door toward the palace.

"Hey, am I glad to see you!" Jacen said, opening the door to find Peckhum standing there bedraggled and distraught. "Do you know where Zekk is? Have you seen him? Have you heard from him?"

Peckhum's face gave Jacen his answer. "I was hoping maybe you'd have some news for *me*," the old spacer said.

Suddenly remembering his manners, Jacen gestured Peckhum inside. "Uh, sorry. Come on in. I'll get Jaina and the others."

His sister and Lowie were at work plotting orbital debris patterns in their holo simulation, while Tenel Ka polished the weapons at her belt.

"Hey," Jacen said, "Peckhum's here, and he says he doesn't know where Zekk is either."

His sister's intent expression turned to one of concern. Lowie scrambled to his feet and pulled Jaina to hers. Back in the living area, all five of them reviewed a map of Imperial City, bending over a projection while Tenel Ka indicated several highlighted blocks of skyscrapers. "We have searched this area near your home," she told Peckhum.

Jacen crowded next to the image. "And we

went to some of the places Zekk took us when we were scavenger hunting," he added. "The ones we could find our way back to, that is."

Peckhum nodded, scratching at his stubble, a distracted look on his face.

"Anakin and Threepio even went to a couple of the places that Zekk had talked about— didn't find anything," Jaina said. "We'd hoped you could offer us some other suggestions about where to look."

Lowie rumbled a comment, and Em Teedee said, "Master Lowbacca wishes to point out that our lack of familiarity with the, shall we say, 'less savory' aspects of Imperial City is, perhaps, an impediment to our search." The Wookiee growled at this overblown translation, but made no further comment.

"He's right, you know," Jaina said. "We really only know the good parts of the city."

Tenel Ka added, "And we were not absolutely certain until now that Zekk was missing. Your observations make it more definite."

"Hey, now that Peckhum's back, and we know for sure that Zekk's missing," Jacen said, "we can report his disappearance to security."

Peckhum looked up sharply. "No, not security. Zekk wouldn't want that."

"But he's missing," Jaina pleaded. "We *have* to find him."

Jacen was surprised to see tears spring to his sister's eyes.

"Yes," Peckhum agreed, "but Zekk has had a few . . . 'misunderstandings' with security before, and he wouldn't thank us for calling them in. Don't worry, though—I can probably think of a lot of places you wouldn't have known to check."

"Well," Jacen said reluctantly, "that means we'll have to keep searching by ourselves then, but your ideas will be a big help, Peckhum. I guess it's still up to us."

"Zekk is a tough kid," Peckhum pointed out with forced optimism. "He's been through a lot, and he can take care of himself." Then his voice dropped. "I sure hope he's all right."

14

INSIDE HIS PLUSH new quarters at the Shadow Academy, Zekk awoke feeling oddly refreshed and exhilarated. He had slept deeply and well, as if he had somehow needed recharging. He wondered if Brakiss had placed some sort of drug in his food. Even if that was the case, he thought, it was worth it, because he had never felt so alive or so enthusiastic.

He tried to stop thinking positively, tried to summon up some anger at being kidnapped and dragged off to the Imperial station. But Zekk could not deny that he was being treated with more respect than he had ever experienced before. He gradually began to think of this place as his *room* rather than as a *cell*.

He showered until his body tingled with warmth and cleanliness, then spent altogether more time getting ready than he should have. He didn't care, though. Let Brakiss wait. It would serve him right. Zekk didn't want to be here, no matter how much attention the leader of the Shadow Academy paid him.

He was concerned about old Peckhum and knew that his friend must be wild with worry for him by now. He was pretty sure that Jacen and Jaina would also have sounded the alarm. But Zekk guessed that Brakiss knew how to deal with that. Zekk just had to bide his time until he could come up with a plan.

While he showered, someone had taken his tattered clothes and replaced them with a new padded suit and polished leather armor, a sleek uniform that looked dark and dashing. He looked around for his old outfit, not wanting to accept more of the Second Imperium's hospitality than necessary, but he found nothing else to wear—and the fine new clothes fit perfectly. . . .

Zekk tried his door, expecting to find it sealed, and was surprised when it slid open at his command. He stepped out to find Brakiss waiting in the corridor. The calm man's silvery robes pooled around him, as if knit from shimmering shadows.

A smile crossed Brakiss's sculpture-perfect face. "Ah, young Zekk—are you ready to begin your training?"

"Not really," Zekk muttered, "but I don't suppose it makes any difference."

"It makes a difference," Brakiss said. "It means I haven't explained well enough just what I can do for you. But if you'll open a chink in the wall of your resistance—just to listen— perhaps you will be convinced."

"And what if I'm not convinced?" Zekk said with more defiance than he felt.

Brakiss shrugged. "Then I will have failed. What more can I say?"

Zekk didn't press the point, wondering if he would be killed if he didn't fall in with the plans of the Second Imperium.

"Come to my office," Brakiss said, and led the boy down the curving, smooth-walled corridors. They seemed to be alone, but Zekk noticed armed stormtroopers standing in doorways at rigid attention, ready to offer assistance if Brakiss encountered any problems. Zekk stifled a smile at the mere thought of *him* posing a threat to Brakiss.

The Academy leader's private chamber seemed as dark as space. The walls were made of black transparisteel, projecting images of cataclysmic astronomical events: flaming solar flares, collapsing stars, gushing lava fields. Zekk looked around in awe. These violent and dangerous images showed a harsher edge to the universe than the galactic tourism kiosks on Coruscant had.

"Sit down," Brakiss said in his calm, unemotional voice. Zekk, listening for any implied threat, realized that at this point resistance would be futile. He decided to save his struggles for later, when they might count for more.

Brakiss took his place behind his long polished desk, reached into a hidden drawer, and withdrew a small cylindrical flare stick. Gripping both ends in his fine, pale hands, he unscrewed the cylinder in the middle. When the two metal halves came apart, a brilliant blue-green flame spouted upward, shimmering and flickering, but giving off little heat. The cold fire, mirrored on the office walls, threw its washed-out light against the images of astronomical disasters.

"What are you doing?" Zekk asked.

On his desk Brakiss balanced the two halves of the flare stick against each other, forming a triangle. The pale flame curled upward, strong and steady.

"Look at the flame," Brakiss said. "This is an example of what you can do with your Force abilities. Manipulating fire is a simple thing, a good first test. You'll see what I mean if you try. Watch."

Brakiss crooked one finger, and his gaze took on a faraway look. The bright fire began to dance, swaying back and forth, writhing as if it were alive. It grew taller and thinner, a mere tendril, then spread out to become a sphere, like a small glowing sun.

"Once you've mastered the simple things," Brakiss said, "you can try more amusing effects." He stretched the flame as if it were a rubber sheet, creating a contorted face with flashing eyes and gaping mouth. The face melted into the image of a dragon snapping its long head back and forth, then metamorphosed into a flickering portrait of Zekk himself, drawn in blue-green fire.

Zekk stared in fascination. He wondered if Jacen or Jaina could do anything like this.

Brakiss released his control and let the flame return to a small bright point glimmering on the flare stick. "Now you try it, Zekk. Just concentrate. Feel the fire, like flowing water, like paint. Use fingers in your mind to draw it into different shapes. Swirl it around. You'll get the feel of it."

Zekk leaned forward eagerly, then stopped himself. "Why should I cooperate? I'm not going to do any favors for the Second Imperium or the Shadow Academy—or for you."

Brakiss folded his smooth hands and smiled again. "I wouldn't want you to do it for me. Or for a government or institution you know little about. I'm asking you to do this for *yourself*. Haven't you always wanted to develop your skills, your talents? You have a rare ability. Why not take advantage of this opportunity—especially you, a person whose life has had, if I may say, too few advantages. Even if you return to your old life afterward, won't you be better off if you can use the Force, rather than relying on what you once thought of as a 'knack' for finding valuable objects?"

Brakiss leaned forward. "You are independent, Zekk. I see that. We're looking for independent people—people who can make their own decisions, who can succeed no matter how much their so-called friends expect them to fail. You have your chance, here, now. If you aren't interested in bettering yourself, if you don't bother to make the attempt, then you fail before you've even begun." The words were sharp, reprimanding, but they struck home.

"All right, I'll try it," Zekk said. "But don't expect much."

He squinted his green eyes and concentrated on the flame. Although he didn't know what he was doing, he tried different things, various ways of thinking. He stared directly at the flame, then saw it out of the corner of his eye, tried to imagine moving it, nudging it with invisible fingers of thought. He didn't know what he did or how to describe it—but the flame jumped!

"Good," Brakiss said. "Now try again."

Zekk concentrated, retracing the mental path he had taken before, and found it with less effort this time. The flame wavered, bent to one side, then jumped and stretched longer in the other direction. "I can do it!"

Brakiss reached forward and snapped the flare stick together again, extinguishing the flame. Immediately, Zekk felt a sharp disappointment. "Wait! Let me try it one more time."

"No," Brakiss said with a smile that was not unkind. "Not too much at once. Come with me to the docking bay. I need to show you something else."

Zekk licked his lips, feeling *hungry* somehow, and followed Brakiss, trying to squelch his impatience to try again with the flame. His appetite had now been whetted—and part of him suspected that was exactly what the leader of the Shadow Academy had intended. . . .

Inside the hangar bay Qorl and a regiment of stormtroopers worked to unload the precious cargo they had stolen from the Rebel cruiser *Adamant*. Brakiss came in leading Zekk, who stared at all the ships stationed at the Shadow Academy.

"I wish I could show you our finest small ship, the *Shadow Chaser*," Brakiss said with a look of regret, "but Luke Skywalker took it when he charged in here to capture our trainees Jacen, Jaina, and Lowbacca."

Zekk scowled, but refrained from telling Brakiss that it served the Shadow Academy right, since they had kidnapped the three young Jedi first, for their own ends. He looked away.

Up in the control room overlooking the cavernous docking bay, the black-haired Tamith Kai stood watching the activities through slitted violet eyes. Beside her were two dark allies from Dathomir, Vilas and Garowyn. Zekk flinched, his lips curling downward in anger as he noted that these were the ones who had stunned him and taken him from Imperial City.

"Pay them no mind," Brakiss said with a dismissive gesture. "They're jealous because of the attention I'm paying you."

Zekk felt a surprising flood of warmth and wondered if the comment was true, or just something Brakiss had said to make him feel more special.

One of the stormtroopers stopped in front of them and saluted. "I have an update for you, sir," he said to Brakiss. "Our repairs on the upper docking tower are almost complete. We should have it fully functional in two days."

"Good," Brakiss said, looking relieved. He explained to Zekk, "I still find it difficult to believe that a Rebel supply shuttle could have been so unfortunately clumsy as to smash right into the cloaked Shadow Academy! These Rebels cause damage even when they're not looking!"

Qorl hefted one of the small weapons cores from a sealed crate. Zekk guessed from the melted, blackened craters around the control panel that the stormtroopers must have used blasters to break the cyberlocks. The hyperdrive core was long and cylindrical, with yellows and oranges pulsing through translucent tubes where condensed spin-sealed tibanna gas had been charged to power the drives.

"These are fine new models, Lord Brakiss," the old TIE pilot said. "We can use them to power our weapons systems, or we can convert more of our fighters to lightspeed attack vessels, like my own former TIE fighter."

Brakiss nodded. "We must let our leader make that decision, but he will be greatly pleased to see this new increase in our military capabilities. Be careful with those components, though," he said sternly. "Make sure that not a single one gets damaged. We cannot afford to squander resources in the Second Imperium's quest to regain its rightful power."

Qorl nodded and turned away.

"You see, Zekk," Brakiss said, knitting his

pale eyebrows together, "we are truly the under-dogs in this struggle. Although our movement is small and somewhat hopeless—we know we're right. We are forced to fight for what is ours against a blundering New Republic that continually seeks to rewrite history and force its chaotic ways upon us all.

"We believe that can only lead to galactic anarchy, with everyone following their own ways, invading one another's territories, disturbing people, neither caring nor respecting the rule of order."

Zekk placed his hands on his leather-clad hips. "Okay, but what about freedom? I like being able to do what I want to do."

"We believe in freedom in the Second Imperium—truly we do," Brakis said with great sincerity. "But there's a point at which *too much* freedom causes damage. The races of the galaxy need a road map, a framework of order and control, so they can go about their business and not destroy the dreams of others in their own pursuits.

"You are independent, Zekk. You know what you're doing. But think about all those aimless people displaced by the changes in the galaxy, beings who have nowhere to go, no dreams to follow, no goals . . . and no one to tell them what to do. You can help to change that."

Zekk wanted to disagree, wanted to refute Brakiss's words, but he couldn't think of anything to say. He clamped his lips together. Even if he couldn't come up with any good arguments against what Brakiss said, he refused to agree openly.

"No need to give me your answer yet," Brakiss said in a patient voice. Then he withdrew the flare stick from the pocket of his robe. "Take as long as you need to think about what I've said. I'll show you back to your quarters now."

He handed the flare stick to Zekk, who took it eagerly.

"Spend some time playing with this, if you'd like." Brakiss smiled. "And then we'll talk again."

15

JAINA SPREAD HER hands in confusion as Peckhum began to describe some of the places where Zekk might have gone. They could spend months combing the underworld of Coruscant, even years, and still never find the dark-haired boy—especially if Zekk didn't want to be found.

"Hang on a second," she interrupted. "Aren't you going to be with us during the search?"

Peckhum shook his head. "New emergency schedule, thanks to that Imperial attack on the *Adamant*. I have to go right back up to the mirror station tomorrow. Thing is, I'm not sure how to keep the systems running without some major repairs. Now even my comm units are down. Fat lot of good I'd be if Coruscant Central calls a red alert. I sure wish I'd gotten that replacement multitasking unit Zekk promised."

Jaina felt a wash of indignant defensiveness

on the young man's behalf. "You know Zekk would've brought it to you if he could."

Peckhum looked back at her with a mixture of surprise and amusement. "I won't argue with that," he said, "but I can't keep my mirror station running unless something gets fixed—pronto."

Lowie spoke through Em Teedee as the three other companions sat restlessly in the open area of Han and Leia's living quarters. "Oh, indeed," the miniature translating droid said. "That's a fine idea." Em Teedee's tinny voice caused the other young Jedi Knights to sit up straighter and look at Lowie. "Why, it doesn't even sound very dangerous."

"What doesn't?" Jaina asked.

"Master Lowbacca suggests that perhaps he and you, Mistress Jaina, along with his uncle Chewbacca—if we can convince him—might accompany Master Peckhum up to his mirror station to see if we can effect temporary repairs."

"That's a kind offer," Peckhum said, "but I don't see how much you could do without a new central multitasking unit."

Jacen snorted. "I can't remember the last time Jaina *wasn't* able to whip up some kind of solution. She could probably fix the whole place using nothing but her imagination."

"Thanks for the vote of confidence," Jaina

growled at her brother. Then, knowing what Zekk would have done, she sighed in resignation and smiled at Peckhum. "He's right, you know. I'm sure we can repair enough subsystems to keep you going until we find Zekk. So what are we waiting for?"

"But why should you want to do that?" Peckhum asked.

"You need the help, don't you?" Jaina asked, momentarily confused. She didn't want to admit that Zekk was the real reason she was doing this. "Besides," she rushed on, "we've been having trouble mapping debris paths in certain areas. Maybe we'll get a better perspective from orbit. Meanwhile, Jacen, Tenel Ka, Anakin, and Threepio can keep searching for Zekk down here in the places you suggest."

"All right," Peckhum said. "You've got *me* convinced, but will your parents agree to it?"

Lowie growled a comment. "Master Lowbacca is confident that he can use his powers of persuasion to convince his uncle Chewbacca to accompany us into orbit," Em Teedee said.

Jaina's eyes lit with confident enthusiasm. "If you can do that, Lowie, just leave my parents to me."

Jacen half-closed his eyes, reached out with the Force, and listened for any sign of Zekk in the deserted building. But he heard only the hollow echo of their footsteps as he and Tenel Ka walked through the gloomy corridor.

He clicked on his comlink. "Hey Anakin—it's Jacen."

"Go ahead," his younger brother answered, transmitting from another building.

"Heading into section seven on the map. Nothing to report so far."

"Okay," Anakin said. In the background, Jacen heard Threepio say in a dismayed voice, "I certainly hope we can locate Master Zekk soon. I'm sure I would much rather be at home than inspecting such . . . unsavory places!"

"I hope we find him soon, too," Jacen said, then clicked off and followed Tenel Ka down the empty hall on the seventy-ninth level of the crumbling building.

The floor was littered with old cartons, canisters, bits of plasteel, and other items too broken-down to be scavenged. Some dry leaves were scattered about as well—though how leaves had come to be in this building, nearly a kilometer below the upper greenhouse levels, Jacen had no idea.

A thin, icy breeze whistled through a crack in the wall, skittering the dead leaves across the floor. The breeze did nothing to dispel the odors of mildew and decay that hung around the old structure, but it did send a chill of apprehension up Jacen's spine. He let his eyes fall half closed again in concentration as he walked slowly along.

Suddenly, something light and warm touched his arm. Jacen's eyes flew open. Tenel Ka's hand rested on the sleeve of his jumpsuit. "I thought you might stumble," she said, pointing at a small pile of rubble ahead of them, where part of the ceiling had given way. In these old buildings, nothing was repaired unless someone planned to use the space. Floors and ceilings were no exception. If she hadn't stopped him, Jacen would have fallen on his face.

"Thanks," he said with a lopsided grin. "Nice to know you really care."

Tenel Ka blinked once. She stood still beside him, not rising to the bait—or perhaps not noticing it. "It is simpler to prevent an accident than to carry an injured companion."

That wasn't the response Jacen had been hoping for. "Well, hey, I'm glad you didn't have to strain any muscles," he said, kicking at the rocky debris with the toe of one boot and sending a cloud of dust into the air.

"It is not a question of strain." Tenel Ka coughed, but her voice remained detached and gruff. "I could lift you easily, should the need arise." She stepped around the rubble. "But I saw no need."

Jacen followed her, wondering why he always managed to make an idiot of himself in front of the calmly competent Tenel Ka. He grimaced. At least if he had twisted an ankle, he might have had the compensating pleasure of Tenel Ka's arm around him to help him out. . . .

Jacen shoved the surprising mental image aside, realizing that Tenel Ka would probably be aghast if she knew the turn his thoughts had taken. Besides, the only thing he should be thinking about right now was finding Zekk.

Using a map on their datapad, they tried to be methodical in their search, concentrating on buildings where old Peckhum said Zekk most often did his scavenging. Walking from one end of the building to another, each of them would reach out with Jedi senses, trying to find their friend, looking for any sign that he had been there.

Once they were convinced Zekk was not close, Jacen and Tenel Ka would take the stairs, a turbolift, or a chute-slide a few floors down, and begin a search of the next level. If they again found no trace of Zekk, they would move to the next likely location, using the aerial cat-walks that bridged the gaps between buildings. Many of these walkways had not been repaired for hundreds of years, and they creaked as the two young Jedi crossed them.

Anakin and Threepio were doing the same in other buildings. Jacen's younger brother was absolutely delighted to have a break from the golden droid's daily tutoring.

As the day wore on, Jacen grew tired. The longer they spent in the murky lower reaches, the more uncomfortable he grew. A sense of urgency stabbed like a needle at the back of his mind. Zekk had been missing for days, and they had to find him—soon. Before long, it would be too late for the dark-haired boy. He wasn't really sure *why*, but he knew that it was true.

They searched dozens of buildings and crossed as many walkways, but found no clues. The deeper they descended, though, the more signs of life they found. Low life.

Creatures scuttled past them to hide in every shadowy corner. When corridors were too narrow for them to walk side by side, the two young Jedi took turns leading. Jacen watched Tenel Ka in the light of her glowrod as she headed down another cramped stairwell into the inky darkness. Her reddish-gold braids bounced slightly as she made her quiet descent.

At one point Tenel Ka faltered, then regained her footing and continued her smooth pace. "Broken stair," she said, turning to point out the rough area. "Be careful."

Just then a dark fluttering shape rose up

behind Tenel Ka with a keening shriek. Instinctively, she whirled and lashed out at the thing, dropping her glowrod in the process—but the more Tenel Ka batted at the creature, the more frantically it shrieked and flapped about her head.

As soon as Jacen understood what was happening, he reacted. "Hold still!" he said, moving toward the squealing creature, which had managed to tangle itself in Tenel Ka's long braids. "It's probably scared of the light."

Tenel Ka instantly held still, though he knew it must have gone against her instincts. Jacen's thoughts reached out toward the struggling creature, sending soothing messages to it. Gradually, the winged rodent grew calmer and allowed Jacen to touch it. Careful not to make any startling movements, he gently disentangled its claws from Tenel Ka's hair. Then, still crooning reassurances to the agitated beast, he set it behind himself in the stairwell and backed away.

He picked up the fallen glowrod and returned it to Tenel Ka. "Hey, are you all right?" She nodded curtly, and Jacen suspected that she was embarrassed at having been unable to handle a small flying rodent without his assistance.

As they resumed their search, he tried to get her mind off the incident. "So, do you know why the bantha crossed the Dune Sea?"

"No," she said.

"To get to the other side!" He laughed out loud.

"Ah," Tenel Ka said, without even stopping to look at him. "Aha."

He had expected her to be more subdued after the encounter with the winged rodent, but she continued at her usual pace. Jacen began to wonder if anything could penetrate her cool confidence. Though part of him admired her fortitude, another part wished that she had been more impressed by the way he'd gallantly come to her rescue.

At the next walkway, it was Jacen's turn to go first. The rickety bridgework was littered with the usual debris of rocks and plasteel. It creaked when he stepped out onto it, high above the ground.

"Be careful," Tenel Ka said from behind him—completely unnecessarily, as far as he was concerned.

"I think we're getting close to that old crashed shuttle," he said, choosing to ignore her remark. "I'm pretty sure it's just on the other—"

The walkway shuddered beneath him, and his heart gave a lurch as metal support struts sheared away with a shrieking noise. He grabbed the rusty rail.

"Hold still!" Tenel Ka called, but it was too late.

With a sound of popping bolts and twisting plasteel, the walkway sagged downward, split in the middle. As if in slow motion, Jacen watched large chunks fall away as the bridge floor beneath his feet tilted at a crazy angle.

A whizzing sounded in his ears, followed by a soft *clank*. He felt himself slide toward the deadly gap and he grasped the railing, but the corroded metal broke away in his hand. He yelled for help, reaching back for anything to hold on to—and felt a strong arm wrap around his waist, then found himself being swept forward. Almost before he realized what had happened, Tenel Ka had swung both of them across the chasm on her fibercord rope and deposited them onto a sturdy metal stairway on the opposite side.

With a creaking groan of protest, the remainder of the bridge gave way behind them and fell in ominous, eerie silence into the deep blackness below.

It wasn't until Tenel Ka released him that Jacen realized they had been clinging together for dear life. After what they had just been through, the metal stairway where Tenel Ka had anchored her rope seemed none too safe to Jacen. Nevertheless, the two young Jedi Knights stood in silence for a moment longer, staring down into the bottomless gap between the buildings.

"I guess we make a good team—always rescuing each other," Jacen said at last. "Thanks." Without waiting for an answer, he turned and climbed down a few steps to a building entrance. Once inside, he sank to the floor in relief, reveling in its comparative solidity.

Tenel Ka lowered herself shakily beside him. In the dim light, her face looked troubled and serious. "I was afraid I might lose a friend."

You almost did, thought Jacen ruefully. But instead he said, "Hey, I'm not *that* easy to get rid of."

Although she did not smile, Tenel Ka's mood lightened. "This is a fact."

They came upon the crashed shuttle less than ten minutes after they resumed their search. When they saw it, they both spoke at once.

"Zekk's been here," Jacen said.

"Something is wrong," Tenel Ka said. Hearing her, Jacen realized that something was indeed wrong. Tenel Ka noticed his hesitation, and stepped forward. "It is my turn to go first. You may wait here, if you prefer."

"Not on your life," he shot back. "After all, I've got to stay close to you—just in case you need me to rescue you again."

"Ah," she said, raising a skeptical eyebrow. "Aha." She entered the shuttle, and Jacen heard her say, "It is all right. No one here."

Following her inside, Jacen saw that while the shuttle was unoccupied, someone had been there recently, picking out the remaining salvage-able items. Tangles of wire and cable snaked across the dusty deck plates. Stripped bolts and broken fasteners lay strewn about. Several access panels gaped open, showing empty spaces that had once housed the shuttle's vital equipment.

"Looks like Zekk may have been scavenging here after all," Jacen said. "That's a good sign."

"Perhaps," Tenel Ka said, lifting a finger to trace the frighteningly familiar symbol that was etched with crude strokes into one of the access panels. "Or perhaps not."

Jacen looked at the fresh scratches that formed a triangle surrounding a cross—the threatening symbol of the Lost Ones gang. Jacen swallowed hard.

"Well," he said, "I guess we know where to look next."

16

STILL DEEPLY WORRIED about Zekk, old Peckhum piloted his battered supply ship, the *Lightning Rod*, out of its sheltered hangar. The New Republic would have provided him transportation if he'd requested it, but Peckhum liked to take his own ship, though even on its best days it functioned less reliably than the *Millennium Falcon*. And it had never been made to carry so many passengers.

Lowie crammed himself beside Jaina into the back compartment, his ginger-furred legs stiff and awkward as he maneuvered his lanky Wookiee body into a seat built for someone little more than half his size. Lowie wished he had the T-23 skyhopper his uncle Chewbacca had given him the day he started at the Jedi academy, but the small craft was still on Yavin 4.

Peckhum had cleared tools and cartons of junk from the *Lightning Rod*'s cockpit—he usually flew the ship alone—so that Chewbacca could ride in the copilot's seat. Chewbacca brought his own tool kit of battered hydrospanners and diagnostics, gadgets he used while working with Han Solo to keep the *Falcon* up and running . . . if just barely.

When the *Lightning Rod* received clearance from Coruscant Space Traffic Control, Peckhum angled upward through the misty clouds at high acceleration until the glowing atmosphere faded into the night of space. Lowie watched, bending his shoulders to stare out the front viewport as Peckhum maneuvered the ship into a high and stable orbit. The huge solar mirrors remained in position like a lake of silver, spreading a broad blanket of sunlight across the northern and southern regions of the metropolis-covered world.

Although the mirror station was temporarily empty because of the emergency switchover of caretakers, the critical solar mirrors could not be left untended. Peckhum's name was next on the roster, and he had to report for duty, whether or not Zekk had run away from home.

Peckhum brought the *Lightning Rod* to dock against the corroded old station, which looked like a tiny speck dangling beneath the kilometers-wide reflector. Chewbacca and Lowie blatted to each other in Wookiee language, expressing their admiration for the huge orbital mirror.

The thin silvery fabric was like an ocean of reflection, only a fraction of a millimeter thick. It would have been torn to shreds had it approached Coruscant's atmosphere, but in the stillness of space the mirror was thick enough. Space engineers had connected it to the dangling guidance station by dozens of fiber cables, gimbaled to attitude-control rockets that could direct the path of reflected sunlight onto the colder latitudes.

With the *Lightning Rod* docked, Peckhum opened the access hatch, which still bore markings from the Old Republic, and they all scrambled through into the austere station where they would spend the next few days.

"Well . . . isn't this cozy," Jaina said.

"According to my dictionary programming, I should think *cramped* is a better word," Em Teedee observed. "I *am* fluent in over six forms of communication, you know."

The metal ceiling was low and dark, strung with insulation-wrapped coolant tubes and wires running to control panels. A single chair sat in the middle of an observation bubble, surrounded by windows that looked down upon the glittering planet below. Old-style computer systems blinked with reluctant readiness, waiting for Peckhum to awaken standby routines and begin the tedious monitoring of the solar path.

Drawn by the spectacular view of space and the planet, Lowbacca went toward the observation dome. He grasped a cold metal pipe that thrust out from the curved wall and bent down to look at the huge ball of Coruscant. High clouds masked the daylight side of the planet, while the darkened hemisphere gleamed with millions upon millions of city lights that sparkled like colorful jewels in the night.

Lowie had seen planets from space before, but somehow it had never struck him how intimate the setting was. Here, high above the world, he felt a part of the universe and apart from it, a piece of the cosmos and an observer at the same time. It was strange to have such a perspective, and it made the galaxy seem both small and immensely large at the same time.

"Don't just stare, Lowie," Jaina urged. "We've got work to do. Our first priority should be to get those communication systems up and running."

Chewbacca roared his agreement, clapping a strong hand on his nephew's hairy shoulder. Peckhum seemed to be working hard to keep his attention on the routine aboard the station, rather than letting his thoughts wander to Zekk. "I really appreciate what you're all doing," he said.

"Happy to help," Jaina offered as she knelt down to poke around in some control panels. "Lowie, you're good with computers. Give me a hand here."

"Oh, absolutely," Em Teedee said. "Master Lowbacca is exceedingly talented when it comes to electronic systems." Lowie growled a response, and the miniature translating droid answered, "Of *course* they already know that. I was simply reminding them."

"Could you please work on the comm systems first? When I try to transmit, all I can really manage is static," Peckhum said, hovering behind them as he pointed out problems.

Jaina's forehead furrowed with concentration. "Sounds like the power transmission is still working, but the voice synthesis encoders aren't doing their jobs."

With everyone standing around, the area was far too cramped to let Chewbacca push his way in, so the older Wookiee hung back and waited. Lowie suspected his uncle was amused to watch the two young protégés working so hard. Perhaps it reminded him of the way he and Han had worked together, fixing things again and again.

"Well," Jaina said, scratching her cheek and leaving a smear of grime from the corroded control panels, "I expect that by the end of today we'll have these comm systems up and running." She smiled brightly at Peckhum, and Lowie rumbled his agreement. "Just a stopgap measure, you understand, but they'll work."

Peckhum shrugged. "Better than what I've got now. I still wish we had that central multitasking unit," he said dejectedly. "Almost as much as I wish we knew what happened to Zekk."

"I'm sure he's all right," Jaina said, but Lowie knew that she was sure of no such thing.

As Jaina tinkered, Chewbacca went to a different part of the station and roared a suggestion. Lowie readily agreed. Since it was getting toward time for midday meal, it seemed a very good idea to get the mirror station's food-processing units up and running. Lowie's appetite was already large, and his mouth watered as he thought of the excellent dishes they could create, even from the meager ration supplies on board.

Em Teedee tsked. "Really, Lowbacca! There you go again—always thinking with your stomach."

Chewbacca roared an annoyed challenge, and Em Teedee's voice became thinner, less emphatic. "You Wookiees," the miniaturized translating droid said in quiet exasperation, "you're all alike."

17

JACEN HAD GOTTEN distracted so many times during their scavenger hunt for the hawk-bat egg with Zekk that he would never have been able to retrace his steps through the labyrinth of Coruscant's lower levels. Tenel Ka, however, led the way with an unerring sense of direction . . . which didn't surprise Jacen a bit.

The buildings drew closer together, became more dilapidated, more ominous. The walls were dark and smeared with sickly discolored blotches that looked like centuries-old blood-stains. Jacen saw the ever-present cross-in-triangle gang symbol chiseled into the duracrete bricks or splashed on with bright, permanent pigments.

"Ah. Aha. We have found the territory claimed by the gang of the Lost Ones," Tenel Ka said, her senses sharpened like a hunter's blade.

Jacen swallowed. "Let's hope we find Zekk soon. I'd hate to overstay our welcome if that gang is in a bad mood again."

"I suspect they are always in a bad mood," she observed. "They may still be angry at us for escaping them before."

"Well, maybe they've got Zekk. We have to rescue him. That Norys guy seems like a bad customer."

Something skittered along the wall behind them, an ugly spider-roach dashing for cover in a clump of slimy moss. At any other time Jacen would have rushed to study the creature, but at the moment he just wanted to be back home and safe in his rooms.

Tenel Ka looked tall and brave as she marched down the enclosed corridor. Jacen wished fleetingly that he had his own light saber, like the one he had used at the Shadow Academy. He knew the Jedi weapons were dangerous and not for play, but right now he didn't want to *play* with one—he wanted it for genuine protection.

Jacen swallowed nervously and moved closer to the warrior girl, keeping his eyes on her dangling red-gold braids. Maybe humor would turn his thoughts from the sinister gang. "Hey, Tenel Ka—do you know the difference between an AT-AT and a stormtrooper on foot?"

Tenel Ka turned and gave him an odd look. "Of course I do."

He sighed. "It's a *joke*. What's the difference between an AT-AT and a stormtrooper on foot?"

"I am supposed to say 'I don't know'—this is correct?"

"Yeah, exactly," Jacen said.

"I don't know."

"One's an Imperial walker, and the other's a walking Imperial!"

Tenel Ka gave a sage nod. "Yes. Very humorous. Now let us continue our search." She narrowed her cool gray eyes as they approached a corner. "Zekk is your friend. You know him best. Reach out with your Jedi powers again to see if you can sense him. These corridors have many twists and turns."

Jacen nodded. He didn't think his powers were strong enough to locate any person specifically—he wasn't sure if even Uncle Luke could do that—but all he needed was a trickle of thought, an impression, a hunch. He and Tenel Ka were wandering blindly so far, anyway, and the slightest inkling would increase their odds over pure luck.

As he concentrated and closed his eyes Jacen thought he felt a tingle, something that conjured up an impression of the dark-haired boy in his mind. He pointed the way before he could have second thoughts. Uncle Luke had always taught them to follow their Jedi instincts.

He hurried to keep up with Tenel Ka as they moved down one hall, then another. The old skyscraper seemed completely empty, oppressive in its silence despite the inhabited levels far above, but Jacen felt invisible eyes watching him from secret hiding places. He trusted his Jedi senses enough to guess that this was not just his imagination.

"We are getting closer, I think," Tenel Ka said.

They heard voices up ahead, and Jacen recognized the timbre of a clear, strong voice—a young man's voice—though he could hear none of the words. "That sounds like Zekk!" he whispered. "We've found him."

Filled with elation, suddenly dismissing all of his ominous thoughts, he rushed forward while Tenel Ka kept pace, advising caution. "Careful," she said just as Jacen turned another corner and ran into an echoing room filled with battered furniture, half-collapsed ceiling beams, and glowpanels wired to the walls as if someone had rigged them wherever it seemed most convenient to connect electrical power. Other doors leading from the large room were closed, some blocked by crates, others jammed on their hinges.

In the middle of the room Jacen saw a young man, emerald eyes glittering in the uncertain light of the haphazard glowpanels. It was Zekk.

His hair, a shade lighter than black, was fastened at the nape of his neck with a leather thong instead of hanging free down to his shoulders. Jacen had never seen Zekk's hair like that. His friend's clothes were also different: clean, dark, padded, as if they were a uniform—and much more stylish than the suit he had worn to the diplomatic banquet for the ambassador from Karnak Alpha.

Sitting on chairs or sprawled on ragged cushions sat a dozen tough, hard-bitten kids, all in their middle to late teens. Most were boys, but the few girls looked wild and rugged enough to take Jacen apart piece by piece, like an obsolete droid.

The Lost Ones.

"Hey, Zekk!" Jacen cried. "Where have you been? We've all been worried!"

Startled from his speech, the dark-haired young man drew himself up, frowning at Jacen and Tenel Ka. His green eyes flashed with momentary surprise and delight, but he quickly masked the expression with a scowl. Zekk appeared to have aged a dozen years in the few days since his disappearance.

"Jacen, now isn't the time," he said in a rough voice.

A brawny boy with close-set eyes and thick eyebrows stood up, glaring. "I don't recall inviting you two." Jacen recognized the bully Norys.

Zekk gestured behind him to calm the burly gang leader. "Let me handle this." Anger showed clearly in Zekk's face as he shook his head at Jacen. "Why couldn't you have left me alone for just a little longer?"

Jacen scratched his tousled hair, completely baffled. When he stepped forward in confusion, Zekk flinched. "Go away," he whispered, "you'll ruin everything!"

The other Lost Ones stood up from their places like a pack of nek battle dogs zeroing in on a target. Jacen swallowed. Beside him, Tenel Ka placed a protective hand on his shoulder, in case they would be required to fight.

"Zekk, it's *us*," Jacen pleaded. "We aren't going to ruin anything—we're your friends."

Just then, one of the corroded doors at the far side of the chamber scraped open. "They are not your friends, young Lord Zekk," said a woman's voice, rich and low. "You know better than that now. They may *claim* to be your friends, but you've seen evidence of just how much they truly value you."

Jacen and Tenel Ka both whirled to see the ominous form of the black-cloaked Nightsister, with her static-charged ebony hair and blazing violet eyes. The upthrust spines on the shoulders of her cloak looked like spears. Two others dressed in similar fashion stood on either side of her: a young dark-haired man and a petite powerhouse of a woman, both of whom looked as rigid as the towering Nightsister herself.

"Tamith Kai . . . ," Jacen acknowledged. "Charming as usual, I see."

"And Garowyn. And Vilas," Tenel Ka said with an astonishing and unexpected expression—a feral smile—on her normally serious face. "So, how is your knee?" she asked Tamith Kai. Her grip on Jacen's shoulder felt tight enough to crack a bone.

The tall woman's face roiled with a thunderstorm of anger. Her wine-dark lips curled down, and she barely controlled her rage at being reminded of how Tenel Ka had humiliated her during the young Jedi Knights' escape from the Shadow Academy. "Jedi brats," she snarled, "you should learn when to leave well enough alone."

"And *you* should have figured out not to mess with us after the first time," Jacen responded in a challenging tone. "Zekk, what are you doing with these clowns? What sort of nonsense have they been telling you?"

Zekk seemed to waver for a moment, but his voice was strong. "They're offering us—all of us—an opportunity. A chance we never had before."

"Like what?" Jacen said, genuinely mystified. "What could these losers possibly offer you?"

"They're taking us back to the Shadow Academy to train us!" the burly gang leader, Norys, said. "Now we'll have our own shot at being powerful."

"But not everybody has Jedi potential," Jacen said reasonably, trying to keep Zekk talking until he or Tenel Ka could figure out what to do.

"*I* do. You would have known that if you'd bothered to test me," Zekk said defiantly. "And anybody who joins us but doesn't have the talent will be recruited into the Imperial military forces, given responsibilities and a chance for advancement in the Second Imperium."

"Oh, Zekk," Jacen said, shaking his head, "those are all lies designed to lure you into dropping your guard—"

"They are not lies!" Tamith Kai interrupted, her melodious voice holding the potential for deadliness. "We will keep our promises. You will all be given equal opportunities, without regard to your social status in the Rebel worlds. The Second Imperium won't judge who you are—only what you do for us."

"Zekk," Jacen cried, "how can you trust them? These are the people who kidnapped me and Jaina."

"Yes," Tamith Kai continued, "and we have

learned our lesson. Highborn noble pups such as you are no more worthy of being Imperial Dark Jedi than any other student." Her violet eyes glared daggers at Tenel Ka.

"Zekk," Jacen whispered quickly, "this is your chance. Trust me on this: You're in great danger. You could escape now. Get away!"

But his formerly happy-go-lucky friend gave him a look that was somewhere between pity and a plea for understanding. Jacen thought he saw a glimpse of the deep sadness that touched the young man's heart.

Zekk said, "You don't understand, Jacen. You can't because you've always *had* too much. You've never wanted for anything. These people"—he gestured toward the evil Nightsister and her companions—"they're offering me something I never had in my old life. With them I have a chance to *be* someone."

"Not *much* of a chance, if they're the ones offering it," Jacen muttered.

Tenel Ka tensed, holding her hands at her utility belt, ready to draw a weapon.

One by one, each of the gang members stood and glared at the two young Jedi. The burly Norys and the other Lost Ones seemed to have been hypnotized, and Jacen wondered if Tamith Kai or the others were using some sort of Force trick to make them more susceptible to insidious suggestions.

Tenel Ka whispered, "Jacen, we must leave while we can still bring help."

Jacen tensed, ready to turn and run. He clicked on the comlink, hoping to signal Anakin and Threepio, but before he and Tenel Ka could sprint to the door, Vilas pulled out a blaster.

"We can't risk any more of your meddling," Garowyn said. "There's too much at stake."

Jacen and Tenel Ka managed to take a few running steps before stun bolts slammed into them from behind. They plunged headfirst into helpless unconsciousness.

18

BRAKISS SEALED THE locking mechanism on the door to his private office, changing the access code to make absolutely certain no one could disturb him. He wouldn't allow even Tamith Kai to eavesdrop on his special communications with the great Imperial Leader.

Brakiss always found inspiration on the walls of his Shadow Academy office, where the exploding stars, broken planets, and cascading glaciers reminded him of the fury locked within the universe. By using the dark side as his focus, Brakiss tapped into that incredible energy and used it for his own benefit, to help pave the way for the return of the Empire.

He set the glowpanels to low as he waited for the contact, checking his chronometer. Speaking with his ominously powerful leader filled Brakiss with both terror and awe, and he was forced to use a Jedi calming technique, though patience was very difficult.

The Great Leader of the Second Imperium had enormous burdens and responsibilities. He was frequently late for his scheduled communications—not that Brakiss would ever dare mention it. The Leader set his own schedule; Brakiss was merely the dutiful slave who knew his place in the grand scheme.

Just as the Rebels depended on the overestimated protection of their vaunted Jedi Knights, so the new Leader would have his own secret weapon: an army of Dark Jedi who could use the dark side of the Force to carve a broad place in history for the Second Imperium.

But Dark Jedi were notoriously dangerous and unstable, prone to delusions of grandeur. Realizing this risk, the Great Leader had taken precautions to protect *himself* from the Shadow Academy. The huge ring-shaped station was riddled with deadly explosives, detonators threaded through the life-support systems, the hull, and thousands of other places that Brakiss neither knew nor wanted to consider. The moment his Dark Jedi gave hints that they might get out of control, the Great Leader would detonate those explosives and end the experiment without remorse.

Brakiss had to show success after success

to keep his powerful master happy—and the Shadow Academy had recently had several spectacular accomplishments indeed.

With a humming sound, the holographic generators in his sealed office activated, and Brakiss snapped to attention. The air shimmered in front of him as a massive image crystallized into focus, transmitted from some far-distant hiding place in the Core Systems. Static rippled along the edges of the gigantic cowled head that loomed over Brakiss, scowling down at him.

Brakiss instinctively averted his eyes, bowing his head in reverence. After performing the appropriate gestures of obeisance, he looked up into the face of the Great Leader of the Second Imperium—*the hooded, wrinkled form of Emperor Palpatine himself!*

Though the holographic image was fuzzy and fragmented from being transmitted across so many systems on the Holonet, through asteroid belts and solar flares and ion storms, the features of the sallow-faced Emperor were unmistakable. Brakiss looked adoringly at the harsh paternal figure. Here was the man who would make all star systems quake with terror until they learned to live again with respect and glory, in the Imperial way.

The Emperor's skin was ravaged with wrinkles

brought on by too deep an immersion in the potent powers of evil. His yellow reptilian eyes blazed from hollowed sockets, and wattles on his neck hung down like the throat sac of a scrawny lizard.

Brakiss knew that the rest of the galaxy thought the Emperor had died many years ago, first in the explosion of the second Death Star, and then six years later in the destruction of the last of Palpatine's clones. But the Emperor's death *must* have been some kind of illusion, because Brakiss could see the transmission with his own eyes. He could not guess how the Emperor had survived, what sort of trick the great man had played on everyone—but with the Force, many things were possible.

Master Skywalker had taught him that.

When he finally spoke, the Emperor's voice was harsh and raspy. "So, Insignificant One, what is your report for today? More successes, I hope. I am tired of failures, Brakiss. I grow impatient to bring about my reign and the Second Imperium."

Brakiss bowed again. "Yes, my master. I have good news to report. We are sending along the hyperdrive cores and turbolaser batteries stolen from the Rebel supply ship, as you ordered. I think your glorious military machine will make efficient use of them."

"Yesss," Palpatine hissed.

Brakiss continued. "Here at the Shadow Academy your new force of Dark Jedi grows more powerful each day. I am particularly pleased that we have uncovered new candidates from the underworld of Imperial Center—exactly as you suspected, my master. No one will notice their disappearance, and we are free to turn them."

"Yesss!" the Emperor said. "I told you it would be simpler to turn candidates whose lives held little hope. It is especially ironic to snatch them from under the very noses of the Rebel usurpers in the government."

Brakiss nodded. "Yes, indeed, my master. We merely offer the new candidates something they need—and they are desperate to take it from us."

"Ah," the image of the Emperor said. He seemed almost—*almost*—proud.

Brakiss drew a deep breath before continuing. "Naturally, many of these new candidates have no Jedi potential, but still they remain eager for opportunities. Therefore, we have begun training one group as elite stormtroopers. They know the underworld of Coruscant very well, and could prove to be effective spies or saboteurs, should we choose to employ them in such a fashion."

The projection of the Emperor nodded inside

his cowl. "Agreed, Brakiss. Very good." A ripple of static flickered across the transmitted image, and the Emperor's voice wavered. "You shall survive another day."

"Yes, my master," Brakiss said.

The expression on the Emperor's ravaged face grew stern. "Don't disappoint me, Brakiss," he said. "I should be most displeased if I was forced to blow up your Shadow Academy."

Brakiss bowed low, and his silvery robes pooled around him. "I would be displeased as well," he said.

The holographic image of the Emperor shimmered, then broke into sparkles of static as the transmission cut off.

Brakiss felt himself trembling all over, as he did each time he spoke to the awesome Palpatine. Exhausted, he sat down again at his desk and began to review his next set of plans, obsessively careful not to allow any mistakes.

19

YOUNG ANAKIN SOLO stood next to the comm unit in the living area of his family's quarters, exhausted from his long and fruitless search, and worried about his brother Jacen. Staring at the darkened screen, he willed a message to come in from Jacen, but he knew that none would come—he could *feel* it.

He and Threepio had returned to their quarters an hour earlier after covering their assigned search locations, but they had heard no word from Jacen. And Anakin knew he couldn't delay any longer.

He turned and walked over to the wall, where the golden protocol droid sat enjoying the refreshment of a brief shutdown cycle. Ice-blue eyes looked into the droid's yellow optical sensors. Anakin gave the droid a tap. "Wake up, Threepio. We've waited long enough. Time to get help."

The optical sensors winked to life, and See-Threepio gave a start of surprise. "Dear me, I couldn't possibly have overslept, could I? I thought we agreed to rest two more cycles before going out to search again. And you have a lesson plan to—"

"I can sense that something is wrong," Anakin interrupted. "Jacen and Tenel Ka haven't come back."

"Well, if you ask me—"

"I didn't," Anakin cut in. "Try to signal them again with your mobile comlink connection."

"I'm sure they're quite all right, but I'll try." Threepio tilted his head sideways and stared off into space for a few seconds.

"Any response?" Anakin asked.

"No, Master Anakin," Threepio replied with greater concern in his voice. "None at all."

Just then Leia Organa Solo entered the room, smiling brightly at Anakin—then frowning. "Anakin, what's wrong?"

Anakin considered how much to tell his mother—after all, they had asked for her help earlier, but she had not believed Zekk's disappearance was anything serious. Now, though, maybe Leia would change her mind when she learned that Jacen and Tenel Ka had vanished as well. The young boy spilled the story rapidly, with Threepio adding sound effects and embellishing with unnecessary comments.

"Jacen would have answered our call if he could," Anakin said.

"Most certainly," See-Threepio added with enthusiasm. "Master Jacen may be somewhat disorganized, but he is *always* conscientious."

Her alarm growing visibly, Leia said, "He would answer—unless he's in trouble." She reached some sort of decision and snapped into action, demonstrating one of the qualities that made her a good Chief of State. "We've got to go find them. Tenel Ka wouldn't let Jacen do anything dangerous. But she probably doesn't think *anything* is dangerous."

Leia ran to a wall panel. "I'll summon a group of guards to go with us. Threepio, can you trace the location of Jacen's comlink?"

"Well, it's certainly not as precise a tracking system as I'd like, but I suppose that by sending a continuous signal and monitoring the feedback from the mobile comlink I could probably—"

"So how close can you get us?" Leia interrupted impatiently.

"I should be able to pinpoint the signal to within a radius of ten meters."

"Close enough," Leia said.

Anakin gave a sigh of relief. "Let's just hope both Jacen and Tenel Ka are still somewhere near the comlink."

"We'll worry about that when we get there," Leia said, grabbing a medkit and dashing toward the door. Guards rushed into position, still not clear on what the emergency was. "Let's go, Anakin. You're part of this rescue, too. Which way, Threepio?" Leia called.

The protocol droid followed as fast as his mechanical legs could move. "To your left, Mistress Leia. We'll need to find a turbolift and take it down forty-two levels."

Anakin tried to picture in his head where they were going, but with little success. "Maybe you'd better lead, Threepio."

Leia, the guards, and Anakin followed See-Threepio as he picked his way across another rickety walkway between two gigantic buildings. The protocol droid seemed to be enjoying his new importance immensely.

The buildings stretched out of sight above and below them. Once, at a spot where the side rail was missing, Anakin lost his footing and nearly fell off the bridge, but Leia instinctively grabbed him. She looked at her son with shock, then hugged him quickly. "Be careful," she urged. "We've *all* got to be careful."

Anakin shuddered. This area had not looked so dangerous on the map. As they homed in on the comlink signal, working through abandoned levels and empty, ominous halls, he noticed a design that appeared with increasing frequency on the grimy walls: an equilateral triangle surrounding a cross.

"I wonder what that symbol means," he said, pointing.

"I am fluent in over six million forms of communication," Threepio said. "Unfortunately, that design is not in any of my databanks. I'm afraid I cannot offer any enlightenment, Master Anakin."

Leia looked at the guards. "Do any of you recognize the symbol?"

One of them cleared his throat. "I believe it's a gang marking, Madam President. Several . . . unpleasant groups make a habit of living down in the untended lower levels of the city. They are very difficult to catch."

"I heard Zekk talking with Jacen and Jaina about a gang called the Lost Ones," Anakin supplied. "I think the gang wanted Zekk to become a member."

Leia's mouth formed a grim line, and she nodded, filing away the information for future reference. Right now, she just wanted to find Jacen and Tenel Ka.

See-Threepio paused to study his readings. "Oh, curse my inadequate sensors—I'm certain my counterpart Artoo-Detoo could have been much more accurate—but I believe that we are now within two hundred meters of their location."

As the group walked deeper into the dilapidated level, the hall became darker and darker. The guards held their weapons ready, glancing at each other uneasily. Leia held her chin up and bravely pushed ahead with greater speed. Threepio increased the brightness of his optical sensors, shedding a soft yellow light directly ahead of them. Anakin kept his glowrod out and ready; it made him feel safer somehow, as if it were an imitation lightsaber.

Threepio made a sharp right turn into a low, narrow passageway, ducking under a half-fallen girder. Even Anakin had to stoop to get under it. "Are you *sure* this is the right direction, Threepio?"

"Oh yes, absolutely certain," Threepio replied. "Remember, we are following a direct path, homing in on the signal. Young Master Jacen may have taken a more roundabout way. We are within thirty meters now."

They finally emerged into a large, eerily lit room with flickering glowpanels mounted haphazardly on the walls. Anakin looked around at the set of rickety stairs leading nowhere, the food wrappers, cushions, and broken-down furniture, and the odd assortment of sealed doors on the other side of the room. "This must be the meeting place of the Lost Ones."

"Oh dear," Threepio said. "Didn't Master Zekk say those gang members were rather unpleasant sorts?"

The room was deathly silent, and the flickering lights made Anakin uneasy. The guards hesitated at the low doorway, pushing their weapon barrels inside. Even though the room was empty, Anakin sensed a lingering feeling of darkness as he entered and began to look around. He nearly jumped out of his skin when See-Threepio cried out, looking down at the floor in horror.

"It's all my fault!" Threepio wailed again. "Oh, *curse* the slowness of my processor. We should have come looking for them much sooner."

In a heartbeat Anakin had scrambled over the makeshift furnishings to where Threepio stood berating himself. Leia and the guards rushed over to join him.

Jacen and Tenel Ka lay crumpled on the floor, side by side, unconscious . . . or perhaps dead.

Quickly unstrapping the medkit, Leia pulled out a mini-diagnosticator and examined the two young Jedi Knights. "It's all right," she said. "They're alive—just knocked out." She ran her cool palm over Jacen's forehead, brushing aside his tousled hair.

Anakin and Leia slowly nursed the two back to consciousness. Jacen came around first, and

Anakin could tell from the look in his brother's eyes that the news was grim.

"Are you all right?" Anakin asked. He shifted gears as he began to put the pieces of a puzzle together in his mind.

Jacen swallowed hard. "Tenel Ka? . . ." he asked, his voice shaky.

". . . is just fine," Leia said reassuringly. "Looks like you two got stunned. What happened?"

Jacen shivered, as though the room had suddenly become colder. "Tamith Kai was here— the Nightsister from the Shadow Academy— along with two of her friends." His brandy-brown eyes squeezed shut, as if he had just remembered something too painful to bear. He groaned. "And they've got Zekk! I think . . . I think he's gone over to the dark side."

Anakin's breath could not have come out in a greater rush if a bantha had just kicked him in the stomach.

"They're going to train him to be a Jedi," Jacen continued. "A Dark Jedi."

Tenel Ka grunted and sat up. "This is a fact."

"There were other kids here, too," Jacen said. "The Lost Ones. I think the Nightsisters took them all—to the Shadow Academy."

Leia shook her head, her dark eyes flashing.

"I think it's about time we did something decisive about that Second Imperium," she said. "That's twice now they've hurt my children."

"Yes, indeed, Mistress Leia! That's all well and good, but we simply must get back home where it's safe," Threepio said in alarm. "Mistress Tenel Ka, are you capable of walking?"

Her granite-gray eyes narrowed, as if she suspected a veiled insult. "I could carry *you*, if I had to."

Jacen chuckled, then groaned as he held his aching head. "Yeah, I think she's just fine."

20

UP ON THE mirror station, Jaina worked with Lowie and Chewbacca to patch up as many of the worn-out subsystems as they could manage. After scraping together the few spare components they could find, they added their own ingenuity to come up with alternative solutions. Although it was impossible for them to program the food synthesizers to create anything remotely resembling gourmet fare, Lowie and Chewbacca did manage to produce a passable midday meal.

Jaina completed the task of reconnecting the communications systems, making it possible to send brief messages, though the transmissions were still plagued with bursts of static. Chewbacca set to work inspecting the life-support systems, the environmental controls, and the station heaters.

Peckhum watched, performing the few duties

expected of him on his monitoring shift. He bubbled over with gratitude, emphasizing again and again how much he appreciated all the effort Jaina, Lowie, and Chewbacca were putting in on his behalf. "If I had waited for the New Republic to get around to fixing these things, Zekk would have been an old man by the time—" Peckhum broke off with a sad shake of his head.

With the major and obvious repairs completed, the young Jedi Knights had little to do while Chewbacca continued poking around. Lowbacca devoted his energies to finishing the orbital-debris plotting that he and Jaina had volunteered to do. Jaina had helped Lowie with the task, but tracking thousands of pieces of debris was just too daunting for her at the moment. Lowie, on the other hand, had extreme patience for a Wookiee, especially around computers. He diligently plotted one blip after another, noting the more dangerous space lanes in the heavily traveled orbits around the capital world.

Jaina glanced at Lowie's three-dimensional map, but soon turned back to the puzzling images on her own datapad. She reviewed file copies of the newsnet videoclips that showed the mysterious Imperial attack on the supply cruiser *Adamant*. On the day after the attack, she, Jacen, and Lowie had easily identified the modified assault shuttle, with its Corusca-gem teeth, recognizing the craft that had been used to kidnap them from Lando Calrissian's Gem-Diver Station.

Admiral Ackbar had verified their descriptions. The theft of military equipment was undoubtedly part of the evil work of the Shadow Academy. From Ackbar's description, Jaina knew that the Imperial in command of the attack had been none other than Qorl, the TIE pilot she and Jacen had tried to befriend near his crashed ship on Yavin 4.

She sighed and shook her head, watching the footage yet again. Jaina had hoped Qorl would see the error of his ways—and though the TIE pilot had trembled on the verge of surrender, the Imperial brainwashing had won out in the end. And now Qorl continued to cause trouble for the New Republic.

She replayed the videoclip of the *Adamant*'s capture a third time. The film, taken by New Republic forces as they'd rushed from Coruscant to defend the supply cruiser, had low resolution. But something about the clip bothered her in an indefinable way, as it had since the first time she'd seen it.

Jaina chewed on her lower lip. "Something just isn't right." She watched the shark-mouthed assault ship appear out of nowhere, while shots from the flanking Imperial ships took out the *Adamant*'s communication arrays and weapon systems. She turned her attention back to the replay—and suddenly sat up with a jolt. She had been watching Qorl's ship—but it was the *other* Imperial fighters that didn't fit.

"That's it!" she cried. "It can't be."

Chewbacca growled a question as he stood up from his cramped position in the control modules for the life-support systems. Jaina focused her attention on the images of the smaller ships, pointing. "I know my Imperial fighters," she said. "Dad taught me to identify every ship ever recorded . . . well, almost every one." She leaned closer to the image. "Those are short-range fighters." She jammed her finger at the image on the screen. "*Short-range* fighters! They had to come from somewhere nearby. Their base is close—hidden somewhere in this system!"

Chewbacca growled a surprised comment. Lowie, wedged into a chair built for humans with his knobby knees thrust high and his arms reaching almost to the ground, cradled his datapad in his lap, studying coordinates of the known items of space debris. He roared his own question, and waved the datapad in the air.

"Attention! Excuse me!" Em Teedee shrilled. "Master Lowbacca believes he has also found something of utmost importance, an inconsistency in the positions of orbital debris. I can't see it myself *since he hasn't shown me the datapad*"—the miniature droid huffed—"but I trust it's something highly unusual for him to become so excited. You really must calm down, Master Lowbacca, and explain yourself."

Jaina rushed with Chewbacca to look at the thousands of dots plotted in the three-dimensional map of space around the planet Coruscant.

"That can't be right, either," Jaina said immediately. She was still puzzled by her own results, and now Lowie had made the mystery even deeper. "It's pretty much the opposite of what we expected."

Lowie barked his confirmation. Jaina sighed, biting her lower lip again. The entire reason for their mapping project had been to discover uncatalogued debris that posed a danger to navigation. Instead of revealing the uncharted hazard that had destroyed the *Moon Dash*, though, Lowie's map of space wreckage showed absolutely *nothing* in the marked zone. In fact, it was more like a forbidden area in space, an island empty of all known debris, as if somehow it had already been swept clear. But they knew the *Moon Dash* had struck something large enough to destroy it. . . .

With a burst of static from the communications system, words filtered across the small, confined space. "Hello! Hello, Mirror Station? Can anyone hear me? Jaina, are you there?

Peckhum perked up. "Well, now we're sure the communications system works."

"That sounded like Jacen!" Jaina rushed to the comm unit and flicked a switch, but was greeted by a flash of sparks from a burnt-out fuse. The sudden heat stung her fingertips. Scrambling, she yanked off the panel face and stared at the singed wires. She probed with the Force, following the path of the short circuit, and rapidly managed to hot-wire the damaged system well enough that she could answer her brother.

The speakers crackled back to life. "—are you there? Jaina, answer me! This is important. We've found Zekk." A burst of static disrupted his next words. ". . . bad news . . ."

"Zekk!" Peckhum hurried forward, leaning over Jaina's shoulder. "Hello?" he shouted into the speaker. "Where is he? Is he all right?"

Jaina tossed her shoulder-length brown hair out of her eyes. "Wait. I haven't got the transmitter back on-line yet." She plucked out a melted cyberfuse and popped in a replacement yanked from her datapad. "That should do it," she said. "Okay, Jacen—we read you. Are we coming through?"

His voice came over the speakers, sizzling and broken. ". . . some disruption, but . . . understand you."

"'What about Zekk?" she asked with an indrawn breath. "He's not? . . ."

"Dead?" Jacen finished for her. The transmission was clearer now, and his voice sounded stronger. "No. We found him—and then Tamith Kai and a couple of others from the Shadow Academy knocked us out."

"Tamith Kai!" Jaina gave a startled cry. Lowbacca roared, and even Em Teedee emitted a squeak of dismay. "But what would she be doing on—"

"They've recruited Zekk and a handful of the Lost Ones gang," Jacen said. "I don't know where they took him, but Zekk seemed to be with them *willingly*. Tamith Kai said she was going to train him to be a Dark Jedi! They're going to the Shadow Academy."

Lowie growled a curious question, but Jaina asked it without waiting for Em Teedee's translation. "But how *could* they train Zekk? He's not a Jedi—"

"Apparently he has the potential," Jacen said. "Remember, Uncle Luke found lots of candidates who never knew they could use the Force. Zekk had a knack for finding things to salvage, even in places where other people have scavenged already. We just never noticed, never put the pieces together."

Jaina hung her head, thinking of all the time they had spent with Zekk, all the fun they had had together, without her ever having recognized his true potential. "So where is he now?"

Jacen's voice became sad. "I don't know," he admitted. "They stunned me and Tenel Ka, then disappeared. Mom and Anakin came to find us, but that was hours ago. They've probably managed to get off planet by now. I have no idea where they might have gone."

Jaina covered her face with her hands. "Not you, Zekk. Not you!" Then she raised her tear-damp face and looked directly into Lowbacca's bright golden eyes. "The Shadow Academy!" she whispered. "Remember, the cloaking device makes the whole station invisible, like a hole in space—just like on your orbital map!"

He snarled in agreement. "Oh, my!" Em Teedee said, too flustered to provide a translation.

Jaina turned back to the comm system. "We know exactly where they are, Jacen." She glanced at Lowie's datapad and the projected map, zeroing in on the empty spot in space.

Jaina shouted into the voice pickup. "Tell Mom to contact Admiral Ackbar. We've got to mobilize the New Republic fleet. Lowie's going to send you some coordinates. We need to strike fast, before the Imperials realize we've caught them in the act."

"Great," Jacen said. "What are you going to do?"

Jaina smiled. "We're going to shine a little light on the subject."

Old Peckhum sat strapped into the command chair in the monitoring station as it dangled beneath the giant solar reflectors, working the outdated attitude adjustment controls. Jaina crouched over the chair, whispering excitedly into his ear. "Turn the mirrors," she said. "Turn, turn, turn!"

"I'm already beyond the maximums," Peckhum said in despair. His jaw was clenched, his neck muscles taut, and beads of sweat glistened on his brow. "These are delicate sheets of reflective material. We'll tear the solar mirrors if we whip 'em around too fast."

Jaina looked out the observation viewports, spotting the New Republic fleet launching from orbit and streaking toward their invisible target. Their weapons powered up as they homed in on the mysteriously empty zone. Before they arrived, Jaina and the others had to expose the Shadow Academy.

Lowie groaned a question, which Em Teedee

translated. "Master Lowbacca wishes to inquire if the focusing apparatus has condensed the beam of reflected sunlight to its full-power configuration."

"That's for sure," Peckhum said. "Once we get this thing turned, we'll really make them hot under the collar."

Hanging in orbit over Coruscant, the big mirrors finally swung into position, focusing their bright beam of condensed sunlight into the empty void. The mirror beam cut a swath through space like a searchlight.

The light should have kept flying across the solar system, but when it struck the empty coordinates, space itself seemed to shimmer like golden smoke. The high-intensity flood of sunlight continued to bombard the cloaked area, finally overwhelming the invisibility shields around the Shadow Academy.

"There!" Jaina cried triumphantly.

The Imperial station rippled into view and then snapped into perfect focus, a large circular ring bristling with spiked gun emplacements and observation towers.

Lowie and Chewbacca roared in unison, and Jaina shook her head. "They were hiding right on our doorstep all along. That's why they could use short-range fighters to attack the *Adamant*. That's how Tamith Kai and her companions could slip down to the city and steal Zekk away."

"Zekk must be aboard the station then," Peckhum whispered. "That's where they've taken him."

"And the Lost Ones," Jaina added.

Chewbacca snarled, then pointed as the exposed Shadow Academy began to move. Thrusters along the equator of its donut shape burned blue-white on one side, nudging it away from the bright beam of concentrated sunlight.

"Turn the mirrors," Jaina said. "We can't let them get away before the ships arrive."

"Oh dear," Em Teedee said. "I do hope our fighters manage to apprehend that Shadow Academy. I'm still exceedingly vexed with them for reprogramming me when we were all taken prisoner there."

Peckhum punched new coordinates into the mirror directional systems, but the sudden acceleration and the change in direction proved too much for the already-stressed silvery sheeting. The long webs of cables that held the great mirror in position tore free, and a wide gash began to open up, spilling a seam of stars and black night through the glittering reflector.

"We can't hold it," Peckhum shouted. "It's too much!" He shook his head. "We could never target a moving object anyway." Then he looked up and moaned. "My mirrors!"

The Shadow Academy continued to accelerate, and Jaina watched the approach of Admiral Ackbar's vengeful fleet, silently urging them to greater speed. But she could see they would not arrive in time.

"The Shadow Academy must already have been preparing to leave," she said. "Of course. They've got Zekk and some other recruits. They've stolen a shipment of hyperdrive cores and turbolaser batteries. They were only increasing their danger by staying here."

Though its ringed shape made it appear unwieldy, the Shadow Academy picked up speed as it headed toward its appropriate hyperspace jump point.

The first of the New Republic ships soared ahead, firing laser bursts at the Shadow Academy. Several shots struck home, leaving dark blaster scoring on the outer hull; the intensity of the solar mirror must have burned out some shields.

Jaina reached out with her mind, searching for Zekk, still marveling at the thought that the handsome, dark-haired street boy might have the potential to be a Jedi Knight. Or a Dark Jedi. She muttered to herself, feeling guilty, "He was our friend, and we never even imagined he might become a Jedi, too. Now it's too late."

As the New Republic ships arrowed toward

their target, firing numerous laser bursts, the Shadow Academy suddenly shot forward with a bright flash of light. Its acceleration stretched space and bent starlines, then it vanished to its unknown hiding place deep in Imperial territory.

The Shadow Academy was gone. Again.

Jaina swallowed a lump in her throat. And this time the Imperials had taken a friend with them.

21

AT THE OBSERVATION windows of the mirror station, Jaina stood next to Lowie, her hands outstretched, as if she were trying to pull back the vanished Shadow Academy—and Zekk with it. But, with the exception of a few New Republic ships, the area where the Imperial space station had disappeared remained stubbornly empty.

She let her arms fall back to her sides. Her eyes squeezed shut against the un-Jainalike tears that had suddenly welled up, and her mind sent out a silent cry. *Don't go, Zekk! Come back.*

In stunned silence, Peckhum leaned against the station wall next to her. His mirrors were damaged, and Zekk had joined the fragments of the Empire. "He's gone," the old man whispered.

When Lowie placed a sympathetic hand on her shoulder, Jaina felt strength and optimism flow back into her, as soothing as cool water to her burning sorrow. Drawing a deep breath, she searched the observation window again for any sign of hope.

A new movement caught her eye. "There!" she said, turning to grab Lowie's hairy arm. "Did you see that?"

Peckhum squinted, and the young Wookiee gave an interrogative growl.

"What do you mean, 'See what?'" Jaina said. "Look—something else is out there, right where the Shadow Academy was."

Lowie's rumbled reply sounded hesitant, but Em Teedee piped up to translate. "Master Lowbacca is loath even to suggest the possibility, but might that not simply be a New Republic ship, or one of the pieces of debris you've been tracking?"

"Absolutely not," Jaina said stubbornly. "Besides, any debris with a path that intersected the Shadow Academy would have been destroyed already—just like that shuttle, the *Moon Dash*."

Peckhum hunched over the comm system. "Strange. That object seems to be transmitting a pickup signal—if I read this correctly, that is."

Lowie's triumphant roar brought Chewbacca from the main stabilizer unit, where he had been attempting manual repairs to the mirror adjustment systems—to no avail.

"Not very big," Jaina said, studying the mirror station's crude scanners. "Small enough to be an escape pod, don't you think?"

Lowie looked up at his uncle, who rumbled a negative.

"Looks more like a message canister to me," Peckhum said. "Speaking of which, the transmitters are working now, so why don't we send a message to the New Republic fleet? They'll pick it up, whatever it is."

"Well, then," Jaina said, "what are we waiting for? Let's raise Admiral Ackbar."

Lowie transmitted the message while Jaina stared at the screen, still hoping.

"Years ago, Uncle Luke told me about one of his first students, a young man named Kyp Durron, who managed to stow away in a message pod." Jaina sent her mind out toward the object, trying to gather tiny bits of information with the Force. But she felt nothing, sensed no presence of her dark-haired friend. She heard Lowie croon a sad note beside her, but even without his confirmation, she knew that they wouldn't find Zekk inside the message pod.

At least not alive.

Jaina bit her lip and tried to look over Peckhum's shoulder as he piloted his old ship, the *Lightning Rod*, back toward Coruscant. Her view was all but obscured by the hairy form of Chewbacca, who took up the copilot's seat and much of the area around it. Thinking about the retrieved message pod from the Shadow Academy—still sealed against the vacuum of space and possibly containing a message from Zekk—filled her with a sense of urgency.

She wished she could tell Chewie and Peckhum to hurry up, that they had to get back immediately so they could be on hand when the message pod was opened. But that would have been foolish, not to mention rude. The two of them seemed to understand her anxiety and had already pushed the *Lightning Rod* to the highest speed its safety limits would allow. In the compartment behind them, the engines made disconcerting clunking sounds. Jaina bit her lower lip.

Lowie sat in thoughtful silence beside her. Only the deep indentations left by his hairy fingers in the foam padding of the arm cushions told Jaina that the young Wookiee felt a tension similar to hers.

As they reentered the atmosphere, Jaina forced her eyes shut and practiced one of Uncle Luke's Jedi relaxation techniques. But it didn't seem to work.

Finally, a gentle thump and the diminishing whine of the *Lightning Rod*'s engines told her they had arrived at one of the landing pads in Imperial City.

Jaina jumped down onto the landing pad without waiting for the exit ramp to extend fully; she couldn't even remember having unfastened her crash webbing or opening the exit hatch. She immediately caught sight of her parents, brothers, and Tenel Ka, who were standing near another New Republic ship that had obviously just landed. The message pod from the Shadow Academy was already being unloaded. Jaina ran toward her family.

"Any sign of explosives or weapons?" Leia was asking Admiral Ackbar as he stood watching his troops perform their duties.

"Absolutely none. We scanned it," he said. "It's clean. No booby traps."

"What about biologicals?" Han asked. The admiral shook his fishlike head.

"Can't be anything dangerous in there," Jaina said, skidding to a stop beside her parents. "It's from Zekk—I can *feel* it."

Admiral Ackbar looked skeptical, but three young voices spoke up at once.

"Hey, she's right."

"I feel it too."

"This is a fact."

"Even so," the Calamarian admiral said, "in the interest of safety, perhaps we should—"

Unable to bear the suspense any longer, Jaina pushed past the two guards who stood between her and the capsule, and activated the message retrieval mechanism. With a small *whoosh* of depressurization, the double panels slid aside to reveal the contents—a device of some sort, a complicated jumble of knobby plasteel parts and cabling.

"What is that?" Leia asked in surprise.

"Stand back!" Ackbar shouted. The guards tensed, as if expecting an explosion.

Han glanced into the capsule and then looked over at Chewbacca and Peckhum, who had come to join them. "What do you think, Chewie?"

Chewbacca scratched his head and gave a couple of short, surprised-sounding barks.

"Yeah, looks like that to me, too," Han agreed.

"So what is it?" Jacen asked, exasperated at being unable to follow the interchange.

"A central multitasking unit, of course," Jaina whispered in amazement and delight. "From Zekk."

Jaina heard a satisfied grunt from behind her. Old Peckhum muttered, "Kid's never broken a promise to me yet."

Then, as if conjured by Peckhum's words, a holoprojector hummed to life. A tiny image of Zekk resolved itself in the air just above the message pod. Jaina bit down hard on her lip again as the tiny glowing form began to speak. "I'm doing this against the better judgment of my teachers here," Zekk said, "so I'll make this message brief.

"Peckhum, my friend, here's the central multitasking unit I promised you. You always expected only the best from me, and I always gave it. This must be hard for you, but I want you to know that no one has kidnapped me or brainwashed me.

"To Jacen and"—the tiny holographic image hesitated—"and Jaina, it turns out I do have Jedi potential after all. I'm going to make more out of myself than anyone imagined I could be. We were good friends, and I'd never want to hurt you. Sorry I messed up your mother's diplomatic banquet—but that's one reason I'm doing this. I have the chance to become something better—a chance that I was never given by anyone in the New Republic."

Jaina groaned and shut her eyes, but the image continued to speak.

"I know this is something you wouldn't approve of, but I'm doing it for *myself*. If I ever come back, I'll be someone you can all be proud of.

"Don't worry, Peckhum, I'll never let you down. You've been my truest friend, and if there's any way I *can* come back to you, I will."

When Jaina opened her eyes again the tiny image had faded into sparkles, but she wouldn't have been able to see it anyway through her tears.

22

THE HANGAR BAY at the base of the Great Temple on Yavin 4 was quiet and cool, welcoming the travelers back to the Jedi academy. The ship sighed as it settled down on the smooth floor. Luke Skywalker emerged from the hatch and stood in the shadows as his students climbed out after him.

In the days when the Great Temple had been a secret Rebel base on the jungle moon, the hangar bay had been a place of frantic activity, filled with X-wing fighters, noisy equipment, droids, fighter pilots, and miscellaneous weaponry. In recent years, however, this had been a peaceful place of Jedi contemplation.

Luke turned to watch the young Jedi Knights following him out of the *Shadow Chaser*, the sleek Imperial ship he and Tenel Ka had captured from the Shadow Academy while rescuing Jacen, Jaina, and Lowbacca. Luke's thoughts were as troubled as the faces of his young students descending the exit ramp.

With the help of the Shadow Academy, a group of renegades calling themselves the Second Imperium was mounting a serious threat against the shaky peace that had been built over the past two decades by the New Republic. They could all sense it, and the battle was brewing, a great battle that would decide the fate of the galaxy.

The Shadow Academy had become more bold in searching for recruits with Jedi potential. In addition, it seemed to be welcoming trainees with no Jedi skills whatsoever—but why? And then there was the theft of hyperdrive cores and turbolaser batteries from the *Adamant*—components that could be used to build a powerful military fleet. Something big was going to happen—and soon. . . .

Luke had picked the kids up from Coruscant, which had given him an opportunity to see his sister Leia and learn more about the newest Imperial threat to the New Republic. Since then, none of the young Jedi Knights had spoken much, each lost in private thoughts. Now they had arrived back on the jungle moon, where the other students were still training, bringing back the powerful force of Jedi Knights to help strengthen the New Republic. The new government was going to need its Force-trained defenders soon.

Bright sunlight streamed through the broad door of the hangar, bathing the entire bay in light and shadow. Clean shadows. Luke looked up at the sunlight glinting off the burnished quantum armor on the *Shadow Chaser*.

"The *Shadow Chaser* is still a beautiful ship." Jaina's voice cut into Luke Skywalker's thoughts. "Look at those lines, the curves."

"And at least it's one powerful ship the Shadow Academy doesn't have anymore," Jacen added, coming to stand beside them.

Luke nodded. "But it also shows us what our enemies are capable of building. Think of what they can do with that large shipment of hyperdrive cores and turbolaser batteries they just stole."

Lowie grunted agreement. "This is a fact," Tenel Ka said.

Luke turned and strode through the open hangar bay doors, and the young Jedi Knights followed him out into the humid sunlight. Droplets of morning dew still sparkled on the Massassi trees and climbing ferns. The jungle air was filled with the scent of sweet growing things and the croaking, rustling, and twittering sounds of exuberant life.

Jacen's forehead was creased, as if by the

weight of his thoughts. He turned and glanced back into the dimness of the hangar bay, catching sight of the *Shadow Chaser*. He sighed, then finally said what was on his mind. "I still can't believe that Zekk willingly chose to go to the dark side," he said. "Uncle Luke, what are we going to do about him? What did we do wrong? He was our friend, and now he's joined the enemy."

Jaina spoke through gritted teeth. "It's our fault for not showing him that he was just as important as anyone else. We didn't even realize he had Jedi potential. *It's our fault,*" she repeated.

Lowie started to snarl a reply, then quickly reached toward his belt and turned off Em Teedee before the little droid could offer a translation.

"It's not so simple to tell who has Jedi potential and who doesn't," Luke said, sensing Jaina's despair and self-reproach. "Especially if they don't know it themselves. Even Darth Vader had no idea that your mother Leia had Jedi potential, though he spent quite a lot of time near her. You can't blame yourself, Jaina."

Tenel Ka spoke up, a distant look in her cool gray eyes. "Zekk made his own choice for his own reasons," she said. "We all do."

"But how could he betray us like that?" Jacen asked.

Jaina winced at the word. "He can't betray us!" Her voice was hot with the strength of her emotions. "He won't—he promised. And he'll be back. I know it."

"The pull of the dark side is strong," Luke answered. "It's possible to turn away from it, but the price is always high. It cost your grandfather his life. . . .

"But there's always hope—for Zekk, even for Brakiss. We have no way of knowing. One thing I do know, though." Luke turned his face toward the sunlight and enjoyed the feeling of the free breeze ruffling his hair. "The forces of darkness are gearing up for a full-scale war."

"Do we have to just wait for them to make the next move?" Jacen asked. "Can't we try to prepare ourselves for the coming fight?"

Luke looked with pride at each of the young Jedi Knights. "Yes, we can. A great battle is coming," he said, his voice tinged with both sadness and hope. "The Jedi Knights—all of us—have no choice but to prepare for it."

**It's time for the Jedi
to choose their weapons . . .**

**STAR WARS®
YOUNG JEDI KNIGHTS**

Lightsabers

Luke Skywalker has come to a grim conclusion. With the threat of a new generation of Dark Jedi being trained at the Shadow Academy, he knows the New Republic will need all the fighters it can muster. At last, it is time for the young Jedi Knights to build their lightsabers.

But there is more to mastering the ancient weapon than mere swordsmanship. Each student must learn about the mysterious bond between Jedi and lightsaber. For Jacen and Jaina, success will mean growing stronger in the Force. But for one of their friends, failure will mean tragedy . . .

Turn the page for a special preview of the next book in the
STAR WARS: YOUNG JEDI KNIGHTS series:
Lightsabers
Coming in March from Boulevard Books!

Daybreak at last spilled across the treetops on Yavin 4, where Luke Skywalker, Jedi Master, listened to the stirring, rustling sounds of the awakening jungle. The looming stone blocks of the ancient temple had absorbed the deep night's chill and now glistened with dew.

As the morning brightened, Luke wished his spirits could lift as easily.

Cool and stiff, he had been atop the Great Temple for a long time already, sitting patiently in the primeval darkness and thinking. He had used Jedi relaxation techniques to dispense with sleep; in fact, he had not rested thoroughly for some time, so great was his concern over the growing Imperial threat to the New Republic.

Jungle birds cried out and took wing, searching for a breakfast of flying insects. The enormous gas giant Yavin hung overhead, luminous with reflected light, but Luke stared beyond it with his imagination, envisioning all of the galaxy's dark and secret corners where the Second Imperium might lie hidden. . . .

Finally Luke stood and stretched. It was time for his morning exercises. Perhaps the exertion would help him think more clearly, get his heart beating harder, tune his reflexes.

At the top of the pyramid, he went to the sheer edge of the enormous, vine-covered blocks that formed the sides of the towering temple. It was a long drop to the next level, where the ziggurat widened toward its base. Each squared-off set of blocks displayed decorative etchings and crenelations, carved into the stone thousands of years earlier during the building of the ancient structures, weathered by scorching attack and passing time. The dense jungle encroached at the rear of the temple pyramid, embellishing the massive stones with thick vines and overspreading Massassi tree branches.

Luke paused for a moment at the edge, took a deep breath, and closed his eyes to center his concentration. Then he leaped out into space.

He felt himself falling and rotated in midair, executing a backward somersault that brought him into position, feet down, just in time to see the cracked old stones rushing up at him. Using the Force to slow himself just enough for a hard landing, he rebounded and pushed off toward the nearest vine. Allowing himself a brief laugh of exhilaration, Luke snagged the rough jungle creeper and swung up onto the lichen-flaked branch of a Massassi tree. He landed smoothly and ran along the branch without pausing. Next he jumped across a gap in the jungle canopy and grabbed a small branch overhead, hauling himself higher, climbing, running.

Each day Luke challenged himself, finding more difficult routines to continue honing his skills. Even during times of peace, a Jedi Knight must never allow himself to relax and grow weak.

But these were not quiet times, and Luke Skywalker had plenty of challenges to face.

Years ago, a student named Brakiss had been planted in Luke's academy as an Imperial spy to learn the ways of the Jedi and twist them to evil uses. Luke had seen through the disguise, however, and had tried unsuccessfully to turn Brakiss to the light side. After the dark trainee had escaped, Luke had not heard from Brakiss again— until recently, when Jacen, Jaina, and the young Wookiee Lowbacca had been kidnapped. Brakiss had teamed up with one of the evil Nightsisters— Tamith Kai—to form Shadow Academy to train Dark Jedi in the service of the Empire.

Panting from his workout, Luke continued to climb through the trees, startling a nest of ravenous stintarils. The rodents turned on him, flashing bright teeth, but when he nudged their attack instincts in a new direction, they forgot their intended target and scattered through the leafy branches.

He swung himself up and finally reached the jungle canopy. Sunshine burst upon him as he pushed his head above the leafy treetops. Humid air filled his burning lungs, and he blinked again in the morning light. The lush world around him seemed very bright after the filtered dimness of the thick underlevels. Looking back toward the stepped-pyramid of the Great Temple that housed his Jedi students, Luke considered both the new group of fighters he had brought here to help protect the New Republic, and the trainees at the Shadow Academy.

In the past few months, the Shadow Academy had begun recruiting candidates among the disadvantaged young men and women of Coruscant, taking these "lost ones" to serve the Second Imperium. One of these had been the teenager named Zekk, a dark-haired, green-eyed scamp who had been a good friend to the twins, especially Jaina. In addition, the TIE pilot, Qorl—who had spent over two decades hiding on Yavin 4 after the first Death Star was destroyed—had led a raid to steal hyperdrive cores and turbolaser batteries from an incoming New Republic supply ship.

All this and more had led Luke Skywalker to the conclusion that the Shadow Academy was gearing up for a major battle against the New Republic. Since the death of Emperor Palpatine, there had been many warlords and leaders who had attempted to rekindle the Imperial way—but Luke sensed through the Force that this new leader was something more evil than just another pretender.

Bright sunlight fell across Luke, warming his

hands. Brilliantly colored insects flitted about, buzzing in the new day. He shifted against the rough branches and drew a deep breath of the fresh air, catching mingled scents from the lush jungle all around him.

The Shadow Academy was still out there, still training Dark Jedi. Luke hated to rush the training of his own group of students who studied the ways of the light side at the Jedi academy—but circumstances forced him to bring out powerful defenders faster than the Shadow Academy could create new enemies. A fight was brewing, and they had to be prepared.

Luke grabbed a loose vine and let himself drop, *drop* until, landing with a jarring thump against a wide Massassi tree branch, he set off, running at top speed back to the academy.

The workout had awakened him fully, and now he was ready for action.

It was time for another gathering of students at the Jedi academy—and Jacen Solo knew that meant his uncle, Luke Skywalker, had something important to say.

Life at the academy was not a constant series of lectures and classes, as he had experienced during tutoring sessions back on Coruscant. The Jedi academy was designed primarily for independent study in a place where Force-sensitive individuals could delve into their minds, test their abilities, and work at their own pace.

Each potential Jedi Knight had a range of skills. Jacen himself had a knack for understanding animals, calling them to him, and knowing their thoughts and feelings. His sister Jaina, on the other hand, had a genius for mechanical things, electronic circuits, and engineering intuition.

Lowbacca, their Wookiee friend, had an eerie rapport with computers, which allowed him to decipher and program complex electronic circuits. Their athletic friend Tenel Ka was physically strong and self-trained, but she usually avoided relying on the Force as the easiest solution to a problem. Tenel Ka depended on her own wits and strength first.

In his quarters Jacen's exotic pets rustled in their cages along the stone wall. He hurried to feed them and then ran his fingers through his unruly brown curls to remove any stray bits of moss or fodder he might have picked up from the cages. He poked his head into his twin sister Jaina's chambers as she, too, prepared for the big meeting. She quickly combed her straight brown hair and scrubbed her face clean so that her skin looked pink and fresh.

"Any idea what Uncle Luke's going to talk about?" she asked, drying drips of water from her chin and nose.

"I was hoping you'd know," Jacen said.

One of the other young Jedi trainees, Raynar, emerged from his room dressed in an eye-popping display of garishly colored robes with intense primary blues, yellows, and reds. He seemed terribly flustered as he brushed his hands down the fabric of his robe, let out a sigh of dismay, and ducked back into his room.

"Bet the meeting has something to do with that trip Uncle Luke just took to Coruscant," Jaina said. Jacen remembered that their uncle had recently flown off in the *Shadow Chaser*—a sleek ship they had appropriated from the Shadow Academy in order to make good their escape—to discuss the threat of the Second Imperium with Chief of State Leia Organa Solo, his sister and the twins' mother.

"Only one way to find out," Jacen said. "Most of the other students should be in the grand audience chamber already."

"Well then, what are we waiting for?" Jaina said and took off with her brother at a brisk clip down the corridor.

Behind them, Raynar emerged from his quarters again, looking much more satisfied now that he managed to find a robe that was, if anything, even more dazzlingly bright—enough to cause tension headaches in anyone who looked too long. Raynar cinched the robe around his waist with a green-and-orange-patterned sash, then bustled after Jacen and Jaina.

When they stepped out of the turbolift into the grand audience chamber, the twins looked at the restless crowd of human and alien students, some with two arms and two legs, others with many times that. Some had fur, others had feathers, scales, or slick damp skin . . . but all had a talent for the Force, and the potential—if they worked hard to train and study—to eventually become members of a new order of Jedi Knights that was growing stronger with each passing year.

Over the background chatter they heard a resounding Wookiee bellow. Jacen pointed. "There's Lowie! He's with Tenel Ka already."

They hurried down the central aisle, passing other students and slipping between rows of stone benches to reach their two friends. Jaina held back and waited while her brother took a seat next to Tenel Ka, as he always did.

Jacen wondered if his twin sister had noticed how much he liked being with Tenel Ka, how he always chose a place beside the young warrior girl. Then he realized that Jaina would never miss anything of that sort—but he didn't really care.

Tenel Ka didn't seem to object to Jacen spending his time next to her. The two of them formed an odd counterpoint to each other. Jacen always wore an impish grin and enjoyed joking around. Ever since they had met, one of his main goals had been to make Tenel Ka laugh by telling her silly jokes. But despite his best efforts, the strong girl with reddish-gold hair remained serious, almost grim, though he knew she was intelligent, quick to act, and profoundly loyal.

"Greetings, Jacen," Tenel Ka said.

"How are you doing, Tenel Ka? Hey, I've got another joke for you."

Lowbacca groaned, and Jacen shot him a wounded look.

"There is no time," Tenel Ka said, pointing toward the speaker's platform. "Master Skywalker is about to address us."

Indeed, Luke had come out onto the stage and stood in his Jedi robe. His face deeply serious, he folded his hands in front of him, and the audience quickly grew quiet.

"A time of great darkness is upon us," Master Skywalker said. The silence grew even deeper. Jacen sat straight and looked around in alarm.

"Not only does the Empire continue its struggles to reclaim the galaxy, but this time it is using the Force in an unprecedented manner. With its Shadow Academy, the leaders of the Second Imperium are creating their own army of dark side Force-wielders. And *we*, my friends, are the only ones who can stand against it." He paused as that news sank in. Jacen swallowed hard.

"Though the Emperor has been dead for nineteen years, the New Republic still struggles to bring the worlds of the galaxy into an alliance. Palpatine did not take so long to squeeze his iron fist around star systems—but the New Republic is a different kind of government. We aren't willing to use the Emperor's tactics. The Chief of State will not send armed fleets to crush planets into submission or execute dissidents. Unfortunately, though, because we use peaceful democratic means, we are more vulnerable to a threat like the Empire."

Jacen felt warm inside at the mention of his mother and what she was doing with the New Republic.

"In days long past," Luke said, walking from side to side on the stage so that he seemed to be talking to each one of them in turn, "a Jedi Master spent years looking for a single student to teach and guide along the path of the Jedi." Luke's voice became graver. "Now, though, our need is too great for such caution. The Empire nearly succeeded in obliterating the Jedi Knights of old, and we don't have the luxury of such patience. Instead, I'm going to have to ask you to learn a little faster, to grow strong a little sooner. I must accelerate your training, *because the New Republic needs more Jedi Knights*."

From one of the front rows, where he always sat, Raynar spoke up. Jacen had to blink to clear the spots of bright color from his vision when the sandy-haired boy raised his hand. "We're ready, Master Skywalker! We're all willing to fight for you."

Luke looked intently at the boy who had interrupted him. "I'm not asking you to fight for *me*, Raynar," Luke said in a calm voice. "I need your help to fight *for* the New Republic, and *against* the evil ways we thought were behind us. Not for any one person."

The students stirred. Their minds churned with a determination they didn't know how to direct.

Master Skywalker continued to pace. "Each of you must work individually to stretch your abilities. I'll help as I can. I want to meet with you in small groups to plan strategy, discuss ways to help each other. We must be strong, because I believe with all my heart that we face dark times ahead."

Down in the echoing hangar bay beneath the temple, Jacen crouched in a cool corner, extending his mind into a crack between blocks where he sensed a rare red and green stinger lizard. He sent a tendril of thought to it, imaginary enticements of food, dismissing reptilian concerns of danger. Jacen very much wanted to add the lizard to his collection of unusual pets.

Lowbacca and Jaina tinkered with Lowie's T-23 skyhopper, the flying craft that his uncle Chewbacca had given him when he brought the young Wookiee to the Jedi academy. Jacen knew his sister was a bit jealous of Lowie for having his own flying machine. In fact, that had been one of the reasons Jaina had so badly wanted to repair the crashed TIE fighter they'd found out in the jungle.

Tenel Ka stood outside the upraised horizontal door of the hangar bay. She held a forked wooden spear that she used for target practice, throwing it with exceptional skill toward a tiny mark on the landing pad. The teenaged warrior could strike her target with either hand. She stared at her goal with cool, granite-gray eyes, focused her concentration, and then let the sharpened stick fly.

Tenel Ka could have nudged the spear with the Force, guiding it where she wished it to go—but Jacen knew from long experience that she would probably tackle him to the ground if he dared suggest such a thing. Tenel Ka had gained her physical skill through endless practice and was reluctant to use the Force in a way that she considered to be cheating. She was very proud of her own skills.

In the rear of the hangar bay, the turbolift hummed. Luke Skywalker emerged and looked around. Jacen gave up his designs on the stinger lizard and stood. His knees cracked, and his ankles were sore, which made him realize how long he had crouched motionless. "Hi, Uncle Luke," he said.

Tenel Ka threw her spear one last time, then retrieved it and turned to meet Luke. She and the Jedi Master had shared a special bond from the time the two of them had spent together searching for the kidnapped twins and Lowie and rescuing them from the Shadow Academy . . . though Jacen sensed that Tenel Ka and Uncle Luke shared other secrets as well.

"Greetings, Master Skywalker," Tenel Ka said.

The tinny voice of Em Teedee, the miniaturized translator droid hanging from a clip on Lowbacca's belt, chimed out, "Master Lowbacca, we have a guest. If you're quite finished messing up those controls, I believe Master Skywalker wishes to converse with you."

Lowie grunted and raised his shaggy head, scratching the remarkable black streak of fur that rose over one eyebrow and curved down his back.

Jaina scrambled up beside him. "What is it? Oh, hi, Uncle Luke."

"I'm glad you're all here," Luke said. "I wanted to discuss your training. You four have been in closer contact with the Second Imperium than my other students, so you know the danger better than they do. You also all have extraordinarily strong Jedi potential, and I think perhaps you're ready for a greater challenge than the others."

"Like what?" Jacen asked eagerly.

"Like taking the next step toward becoming full Jedi Knights," Luke said.

Jacen's mind spun, trying to figure out what his uncle meant, but Jaina exclaimed, "You want us to build our own lightsabers, don't you?"

"Yes," Luke nodded. "I normally wouldn't suggest this so early, especially for such young students. But I think we're in for a battle so difficult that I want you to be prepared to use every weapon at your disposal."

Jacen felt a surge of delight, followed by sudden uneasiness. Not long ago he had desperately wanted his own lightsaber, but he had been forced to train with one at the Shadow Academy . . . and he and his sister had come close to killing each other in a deceptive test. "But, Uncle Luke, I thought you said it was too dangerous for us."

Luke nodded soberly. "It *is* dangerous. As I recall, I once caught you playing with my weapon, because you wanted one so much—but I think you've learned an important lesson since then about taking lightsabers seriously."

Jacen agreed. "Yeah, I don't think I'll ever think of a lightsaber as a toy."

Luke smiled back at him. "Good. That's an important start," he said. "These weapons are not playthings. A lightsaber is a dangerous and destructive instrument, a powerful blade that can strike down an opponent—or a friend, if you're not careful."

"We'll be careful, Uncle Luke," Jaina assured him with an earnest nod.

Luke still seemed skeptical. "This isn't a reward. It's an obligation, a difficult new set of lessons for you. Perhaps the work involved in building your own lightsaber will teach you to respect it as a tool, as you learn how the Jedi created their own personal weapons, each with special characteristics."

"I always wanted to know how a lightsaber worked. Can I take yours apart, Uncle Luke?" Jaina asked, her brandy-brown eyes pleading.

Now Luke let a smile cross his face. "I don't think so, Jaina—but you'll learn about them soon enough." He looked at the four young Jedi Knights. "I want you to begin without delay."